HAPPY HOLIDAYS

From: Marvel The Avengers

Based on the Marvel comic book series *The Avengers*

Written by Thomas Macri

Illustrated by Ron Lim and Rachelle Rosenberg

MARVEL
New York
Los Angeles

Published by Marvel Press, an imprint of Disney Book Group. No part of this book may be reproduced or transmitted in any form or by any means, electronic or mechanical, including photocopying, recording, or by any information storage and retrieval system, without written permission from the publisher. For information address Marvel Press, 1101 Flower Street, Glendale, California 91201.

Designed by Jennifer Redding

Printed in the United States of America   First Edition   10 9 8 7 6 5 4 3 2 1   ISBN 978-1-4847-1227-6

It was a perfect December night and
New York City was blanketed in snow.

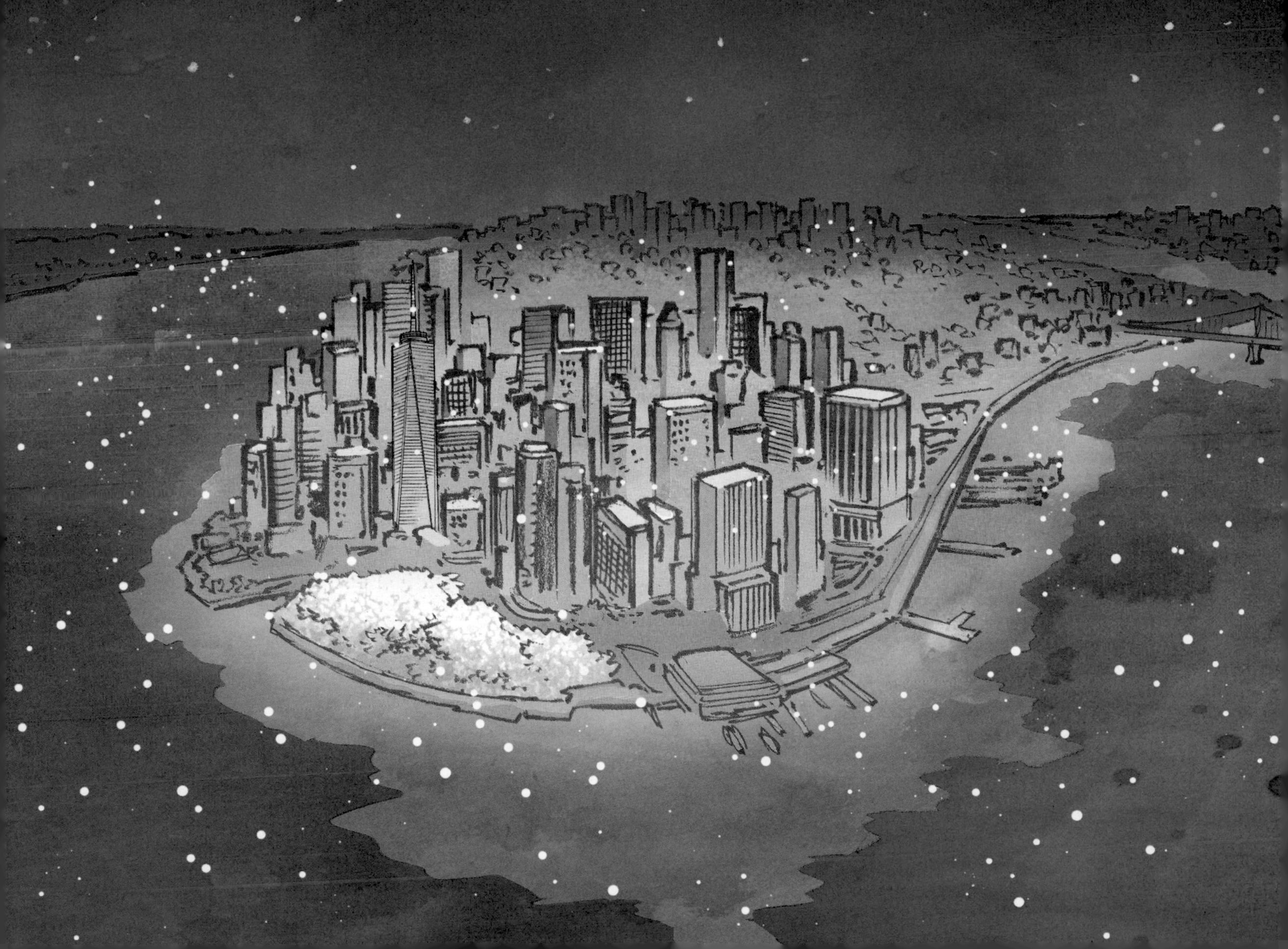

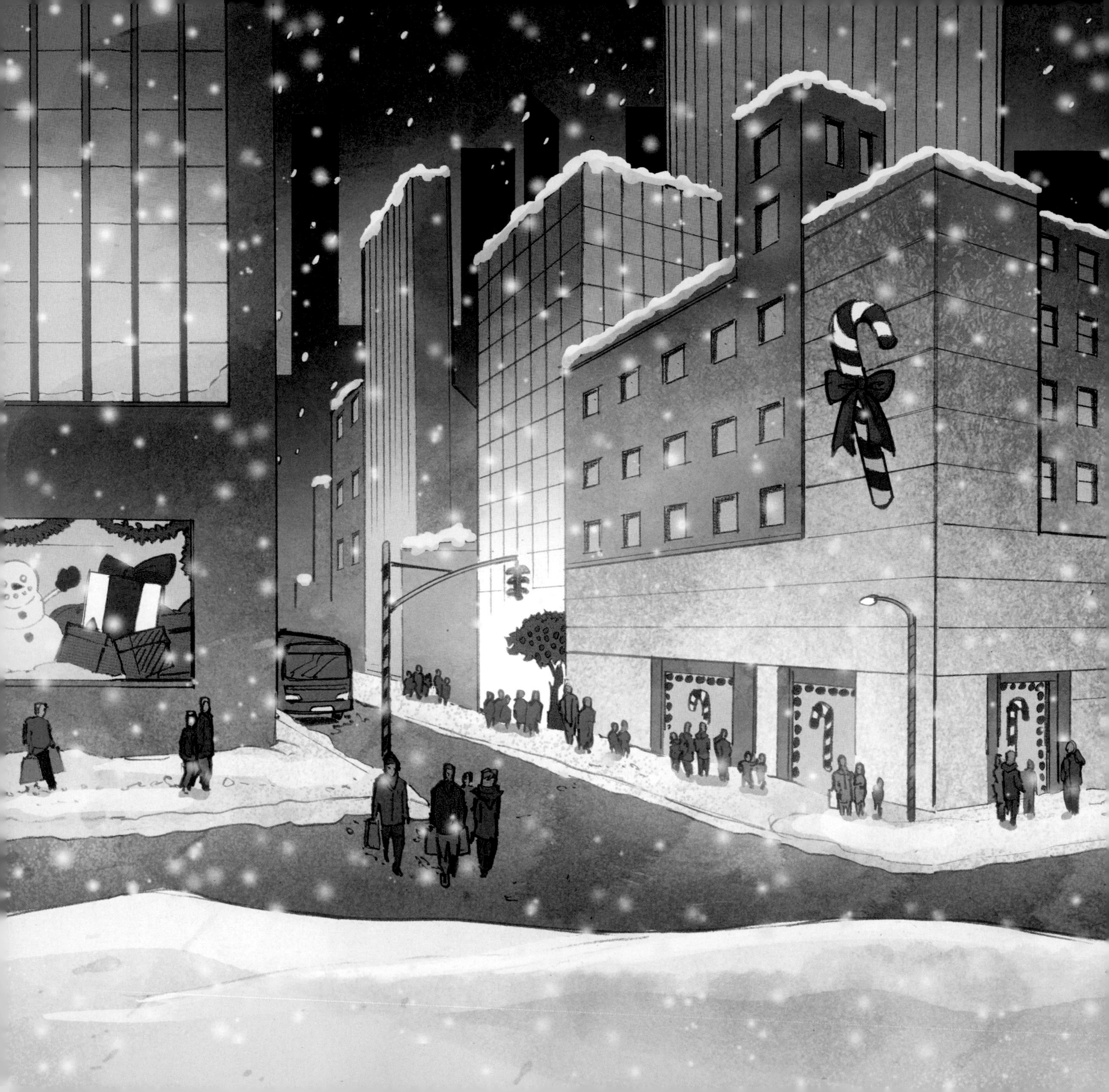

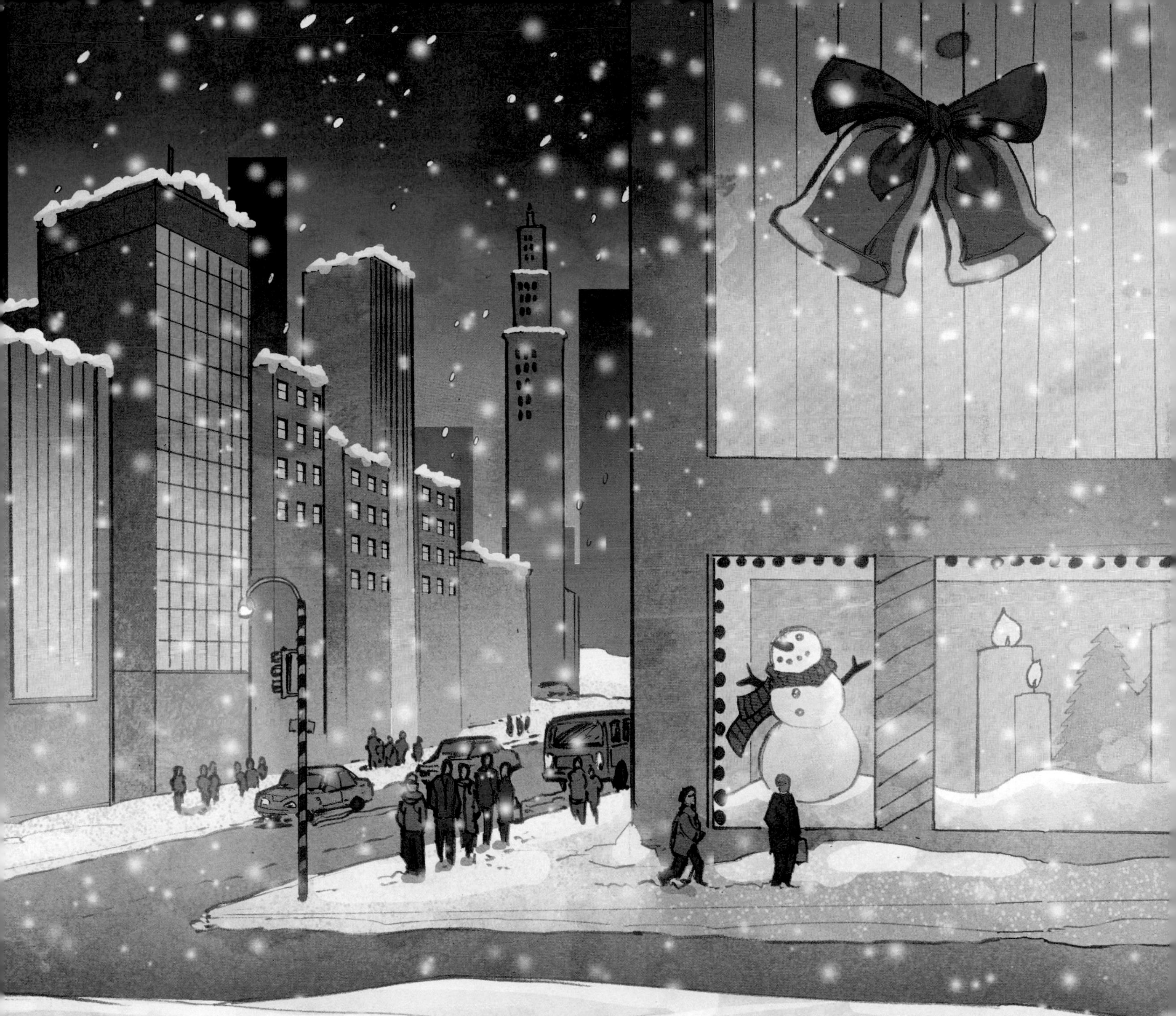

Shoppers hurried to buy last-minute gifts, and people rushed home to spend the holiday with their family and friends.

And the Super Hero team known as the Avengers was no exception. They had all been fighting separate battles and were ready to settle down to a long winter's holiday.

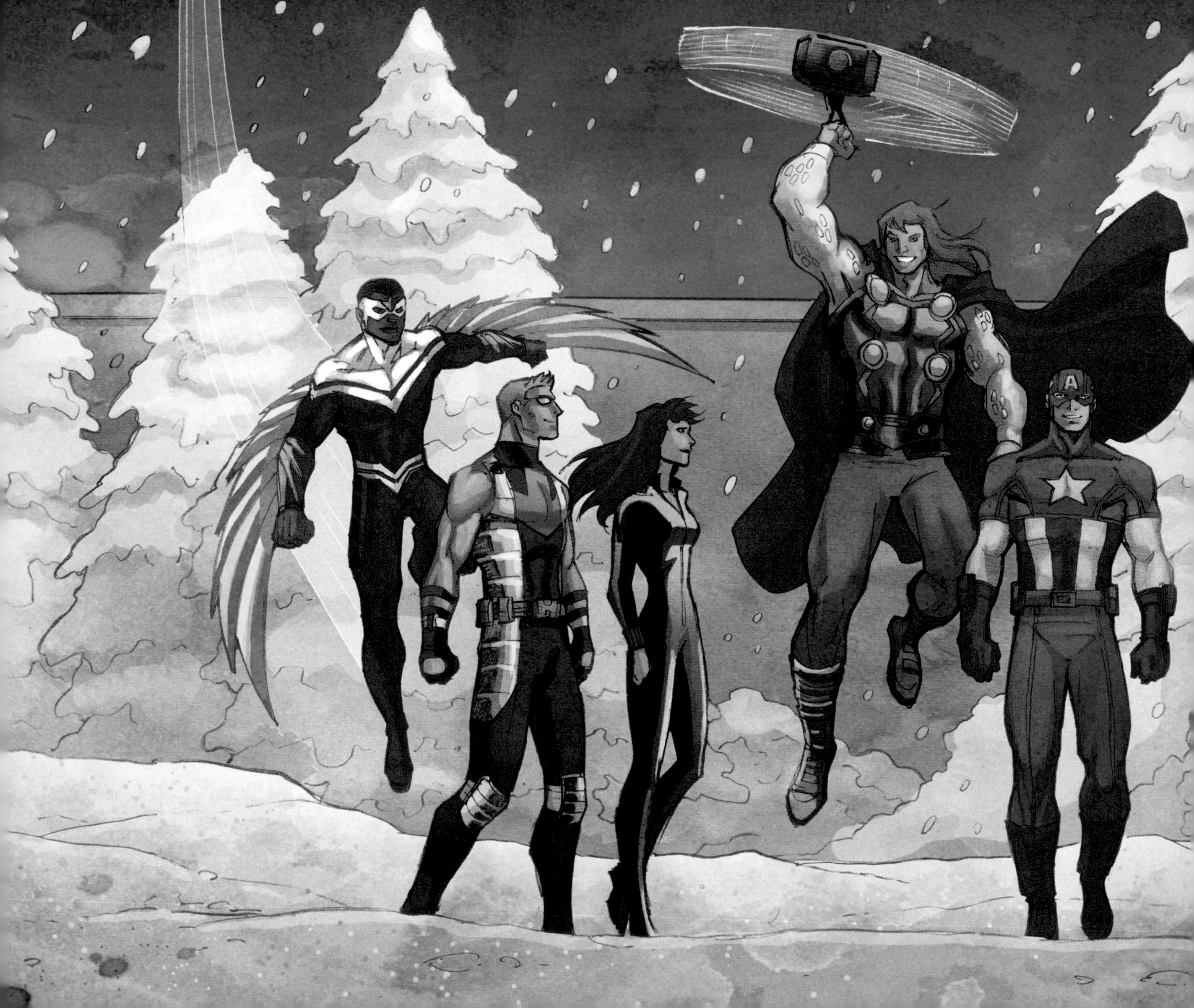

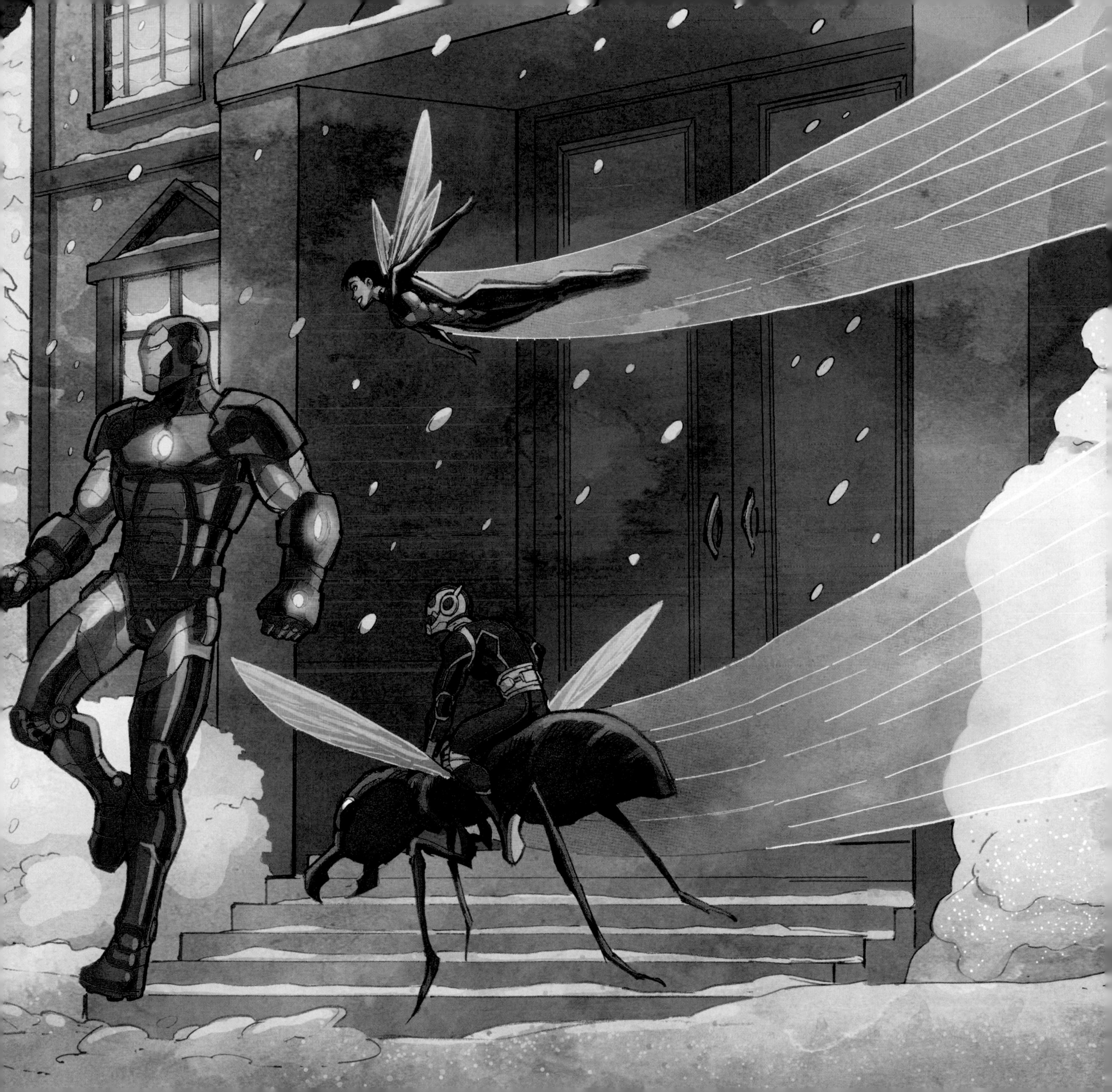

Inside the Avengers mansion, Ant-Man warmed his tiny hands by a flickering candle, while the Wasp placed some festive decorations around the room.

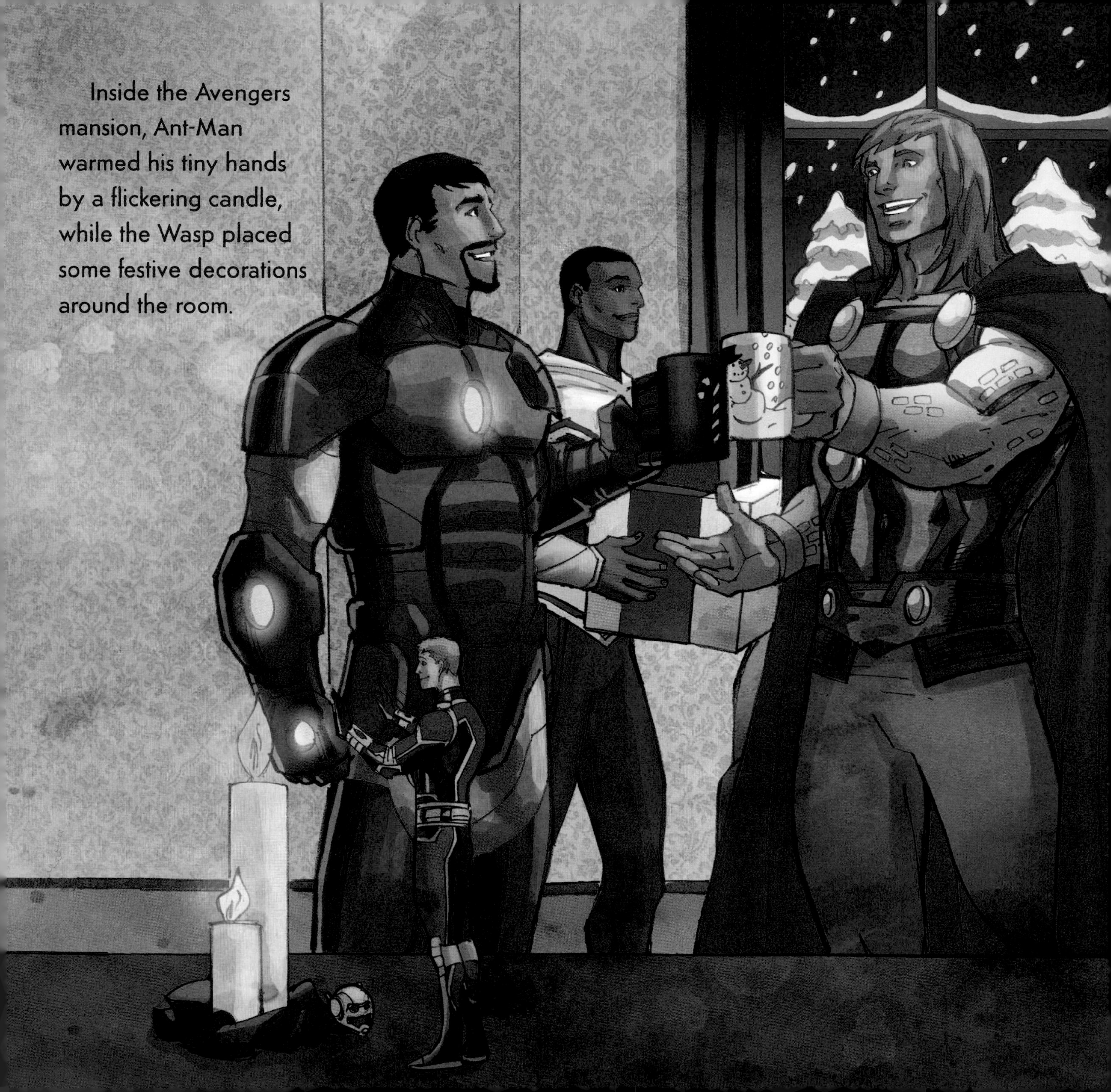

Iron Man and Thor toasted each other with cups of warm apple cider. Captain America and Falcon gathered the gifts they had collected for children in need. And Black Widow and Hawkeye lit up the fireplace.

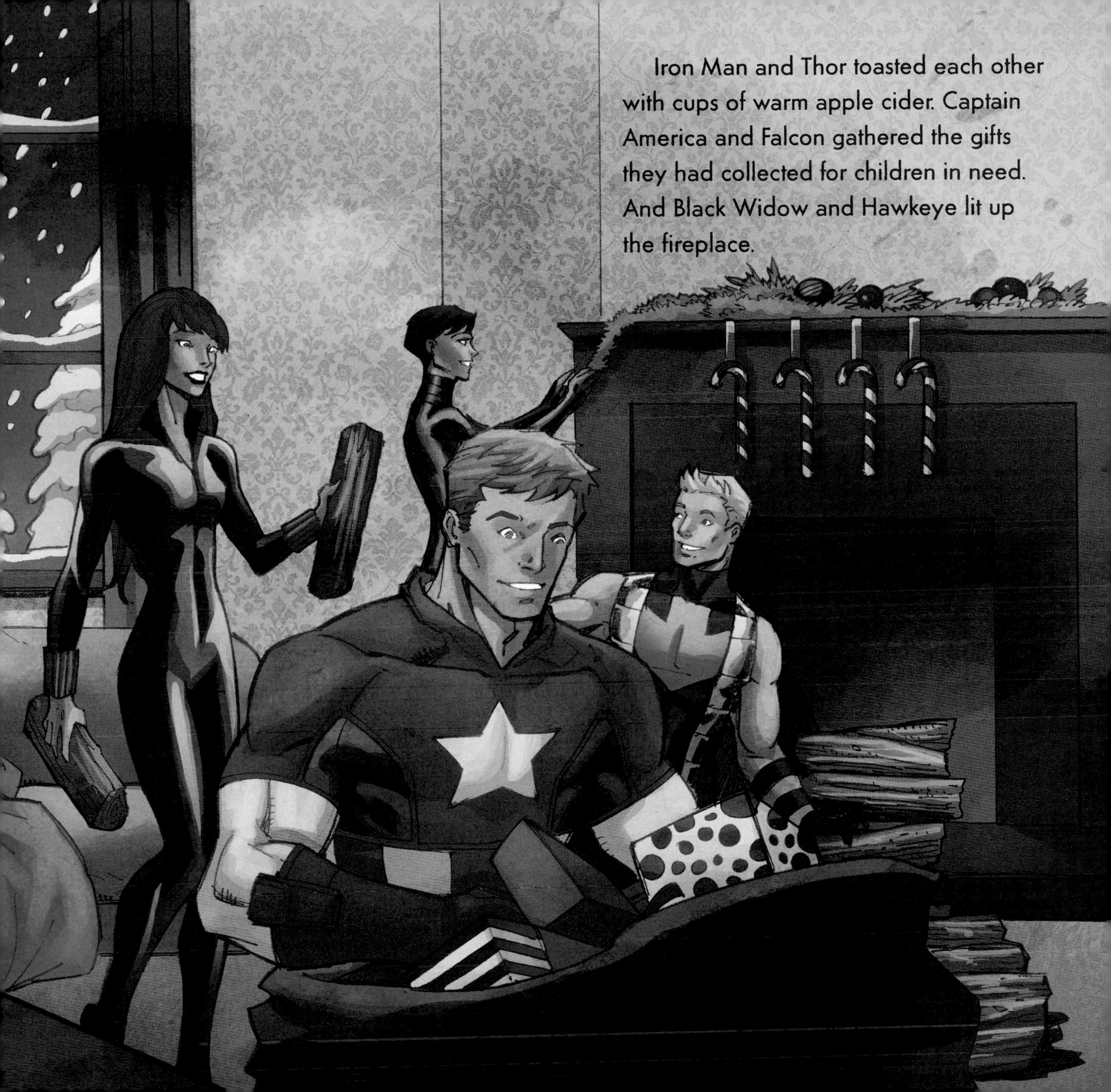

"Wherefore is Hulk?" Thor asked, concerned. "I made him this goblet of hot cocoa to enjoy."

People who don't know the Hulk thought he was a monster just because he was big and green. Even though he was a hero, people feared him because of how he looked.

"He's probably on the run again," Iron Man said sadly. "We'll just have to celebrate without him."

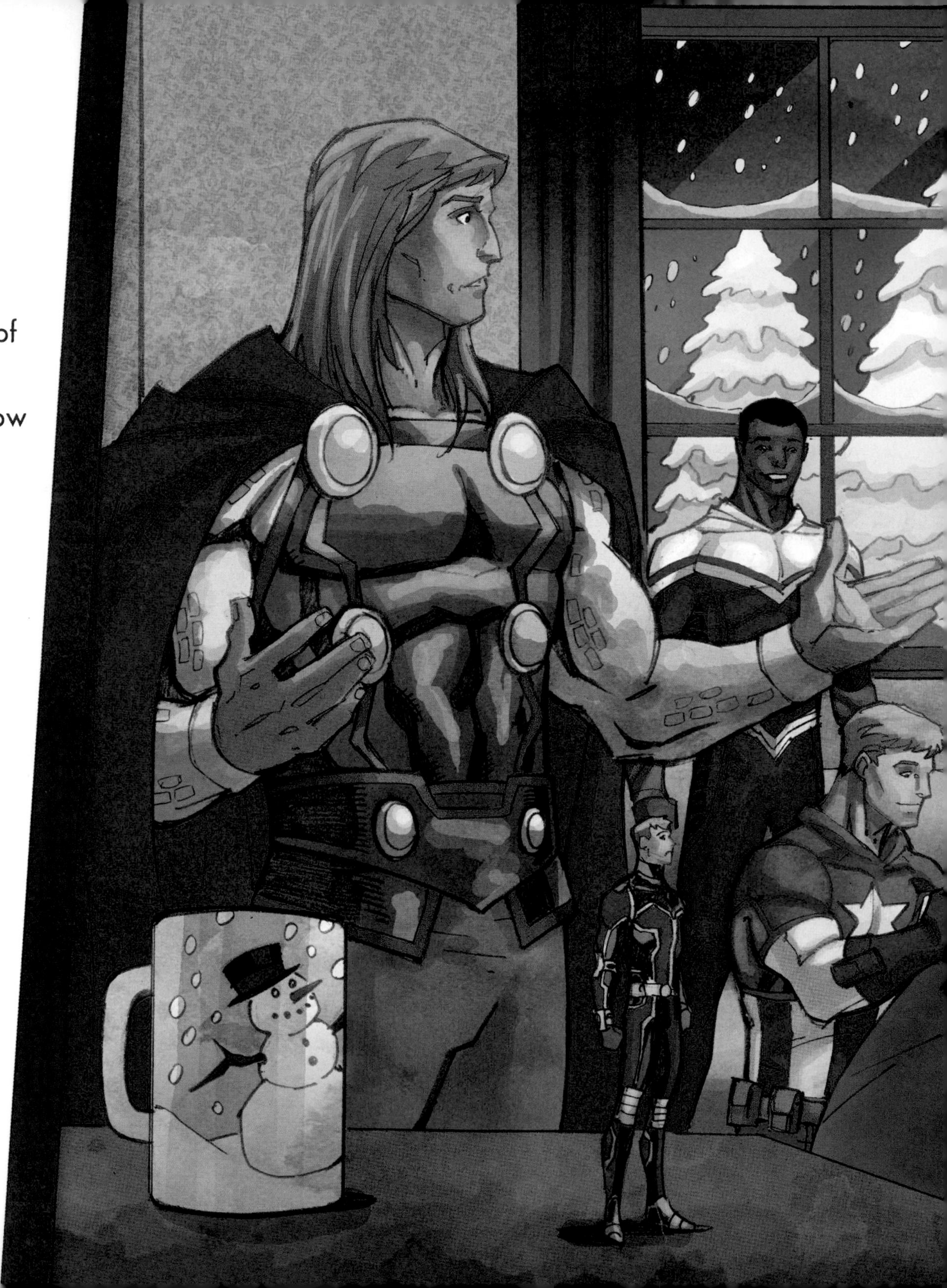

"I guess we will," Wasp sighed, "but the holidays just aren't the same without the whole team here."

Everyone agreed.

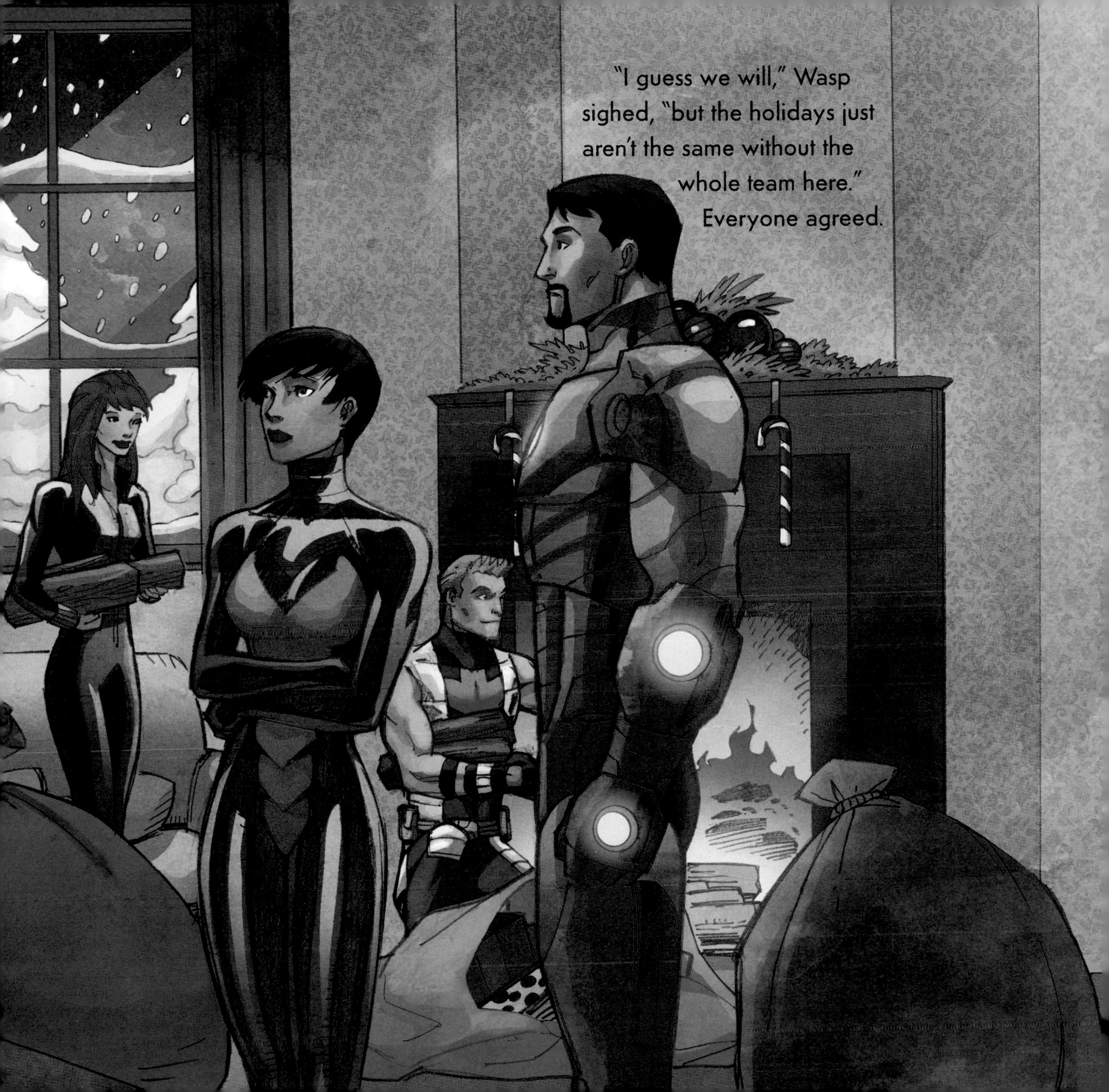

"Well, what are we waiting for?" Ant-Man shouted, trying to lighten the mood. "Let's exchange some gifts!"

"These are from me," Wasp said. "Here, Clint, this is for you." She smiled proudly as she handed Hawkeye a fashionably wrapped gift.

"Thanks, Janet," Hawkeye said to Wasp.

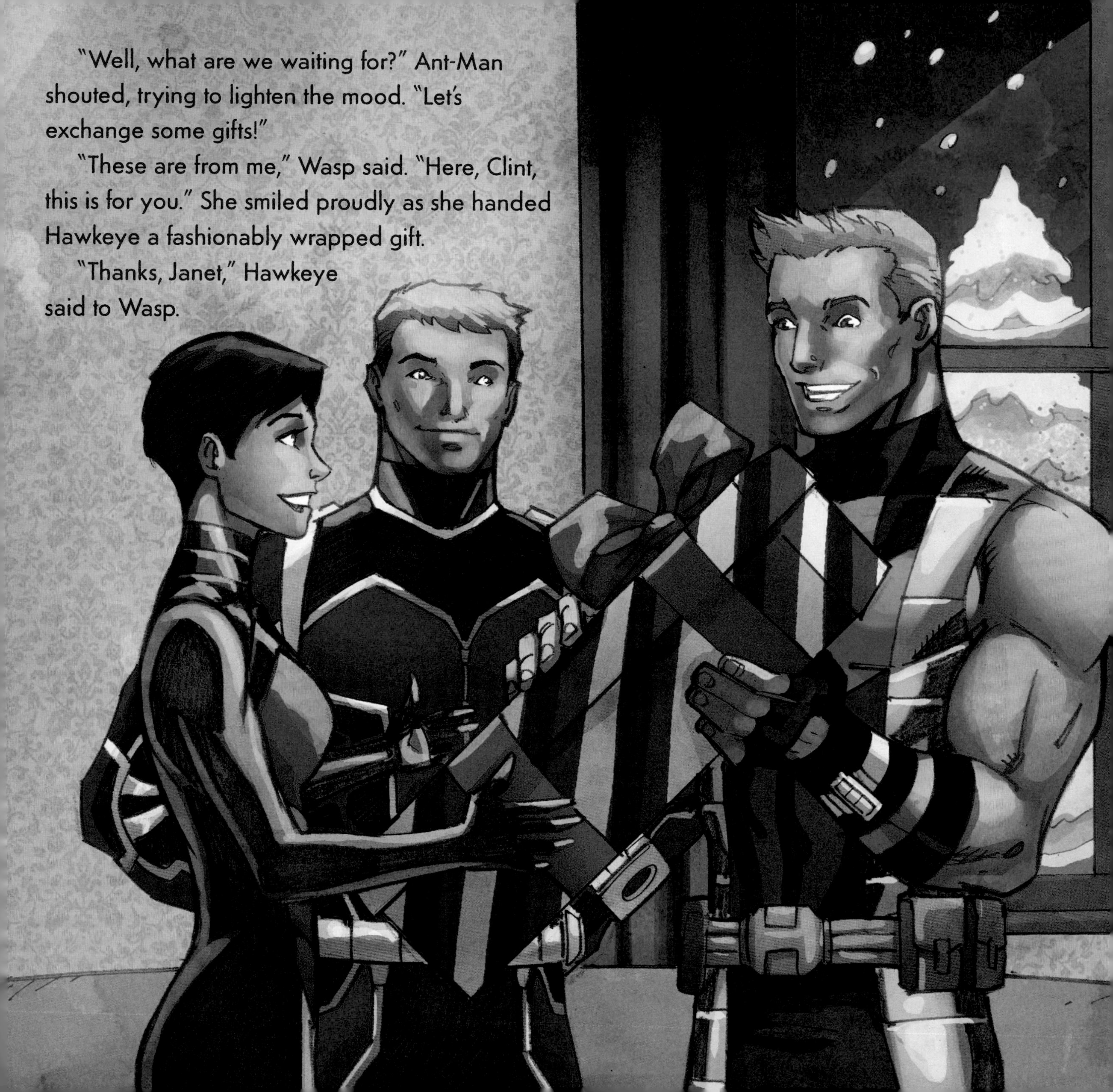

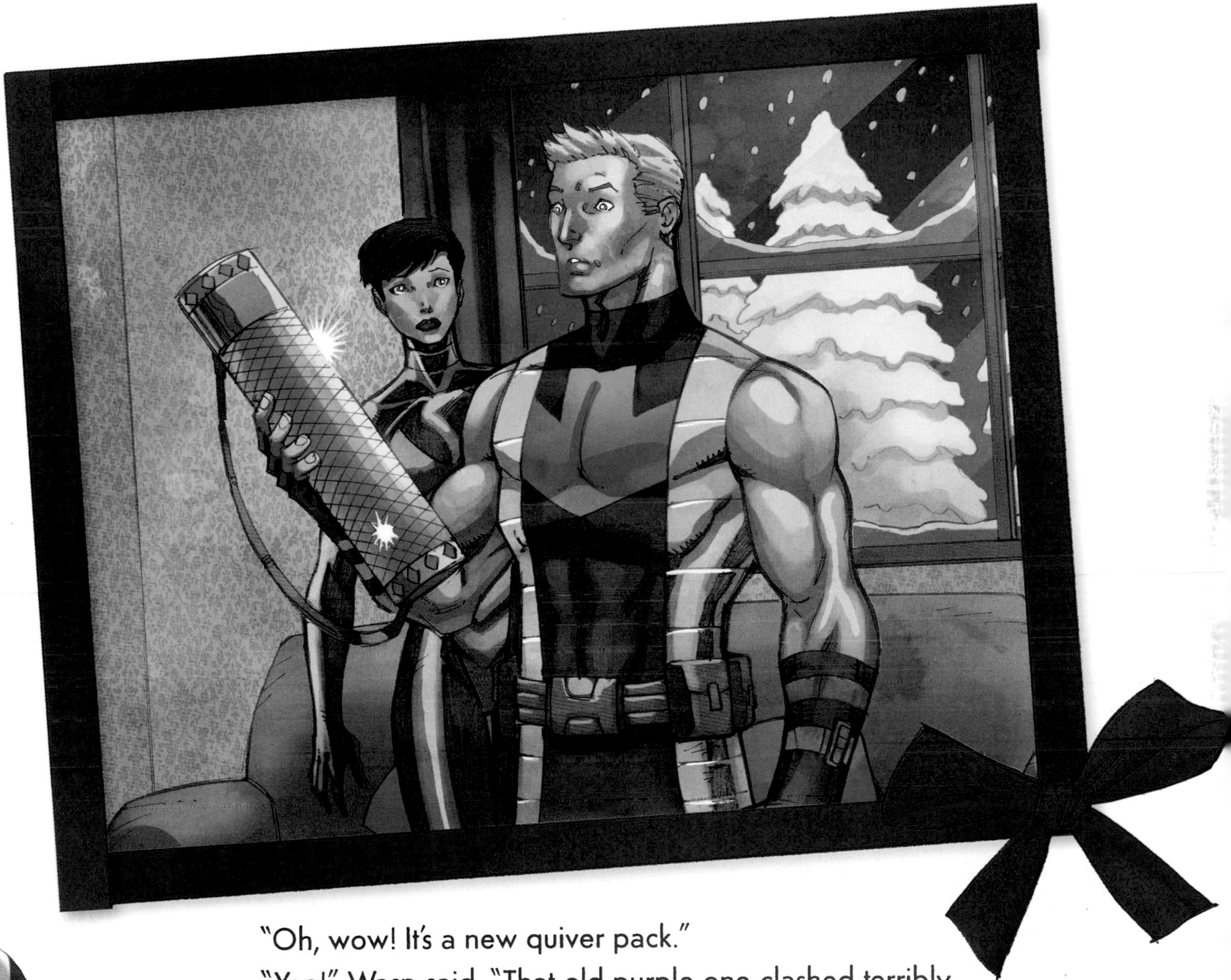

"Oh, wow! It's a new quiver pack."

"Yep!" Wasp said. "That old purple one clashed terribly with your costume. Try it on! Let's see how it looks."

"Uh—Why don't we open more gifts first?" Hawkeye said, quickly pushing aside the quiver pack.

Wasp frowned. "Um. . .okay!"

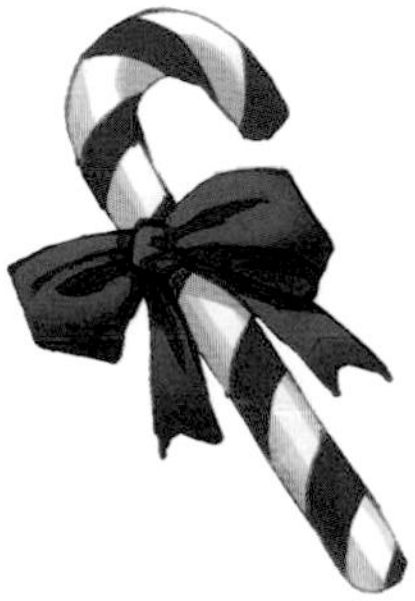

"Okay. Thor, this one's for you, and Cap, this is yours!" Janet said.

Cap and Thor eagerly opened their gifts. But their joy quickly disappeared.

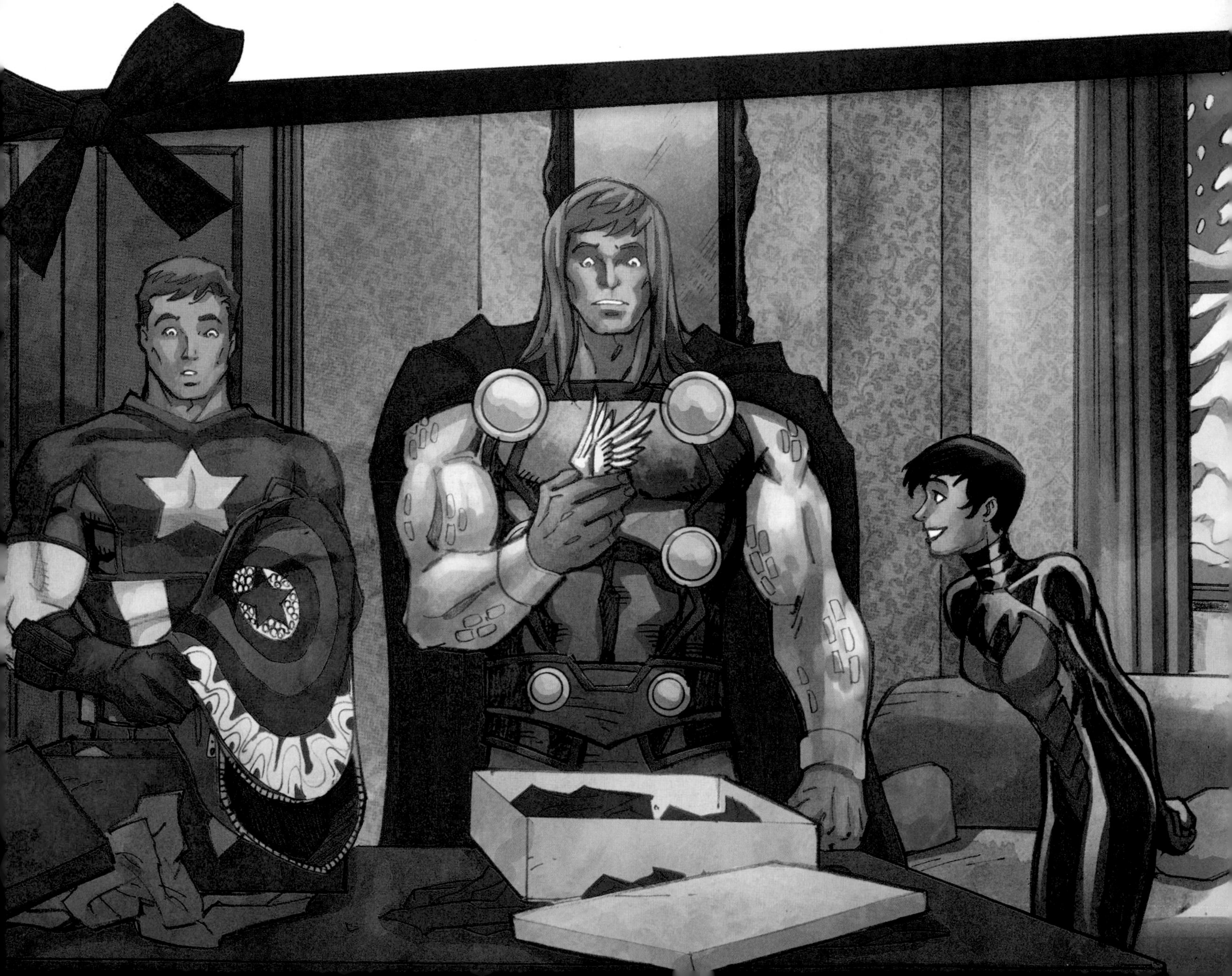

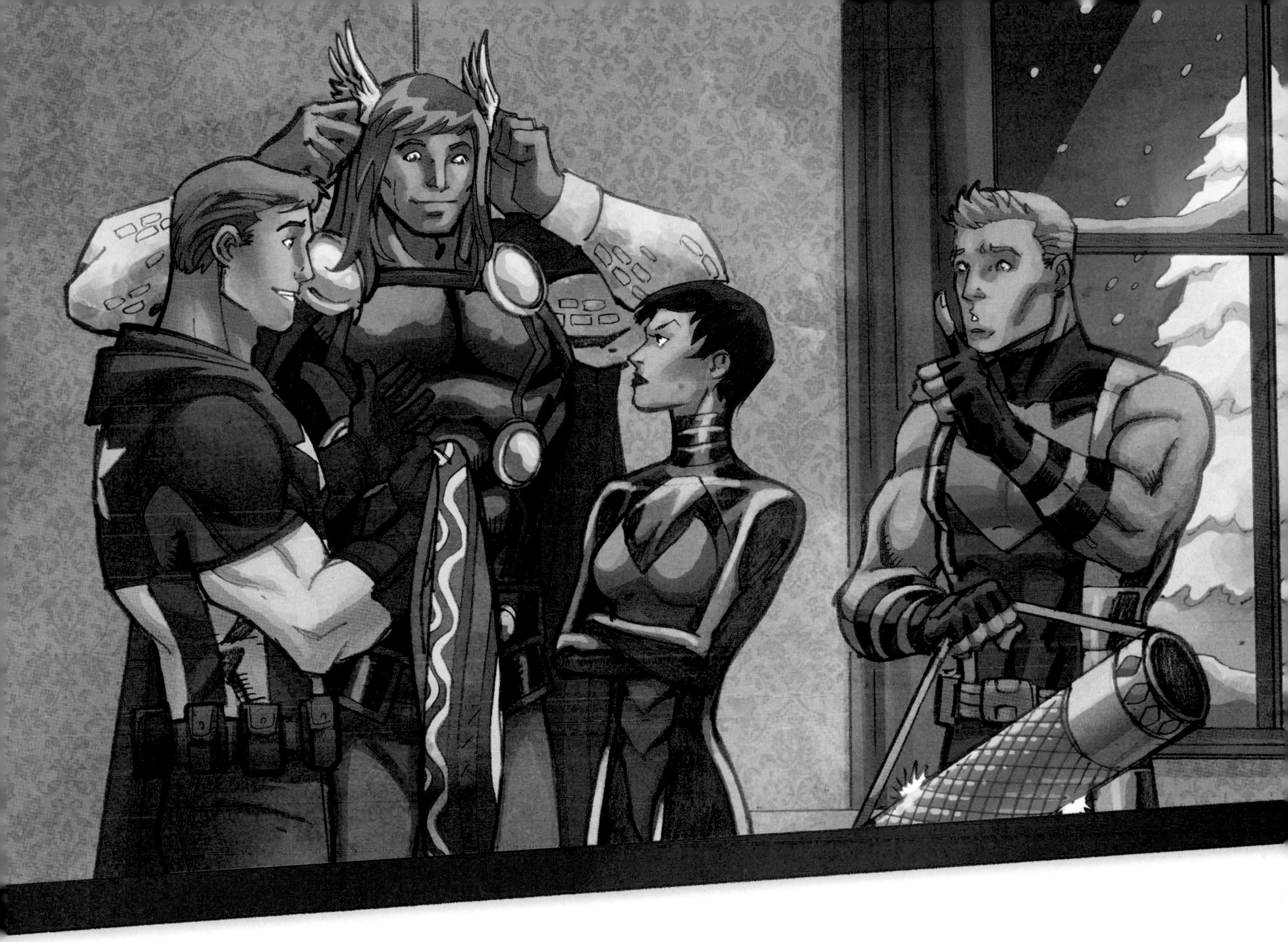

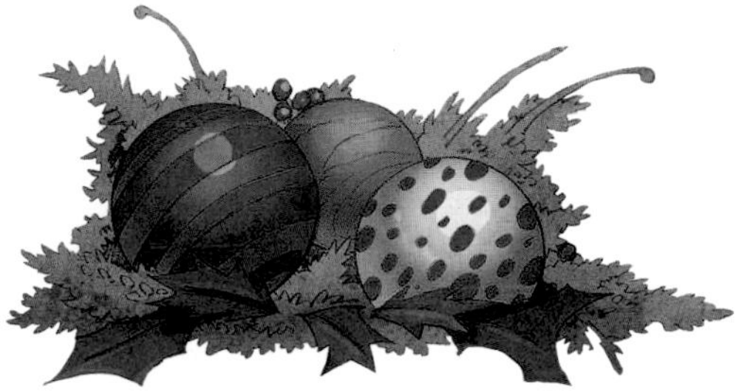

"Oh! Wings! Thou shouldn't have!" Thor said with fake excitement.

Wasp smiled. "They're for your helmet! Those old ones were way too big and made your head look small. And, Cap, that new bag is for you to carry around your shield! That old brown shoulder sack is *sooo* last week."

"Why don't we just keep going? We're sort of on a roll here," Iron Man said.

Wasp sighed and continued. "Okay. Tony, this is yours. Natasha, here, this one's for you. And here's yours, Sam."

She was clearly losing interest in the gift giving.

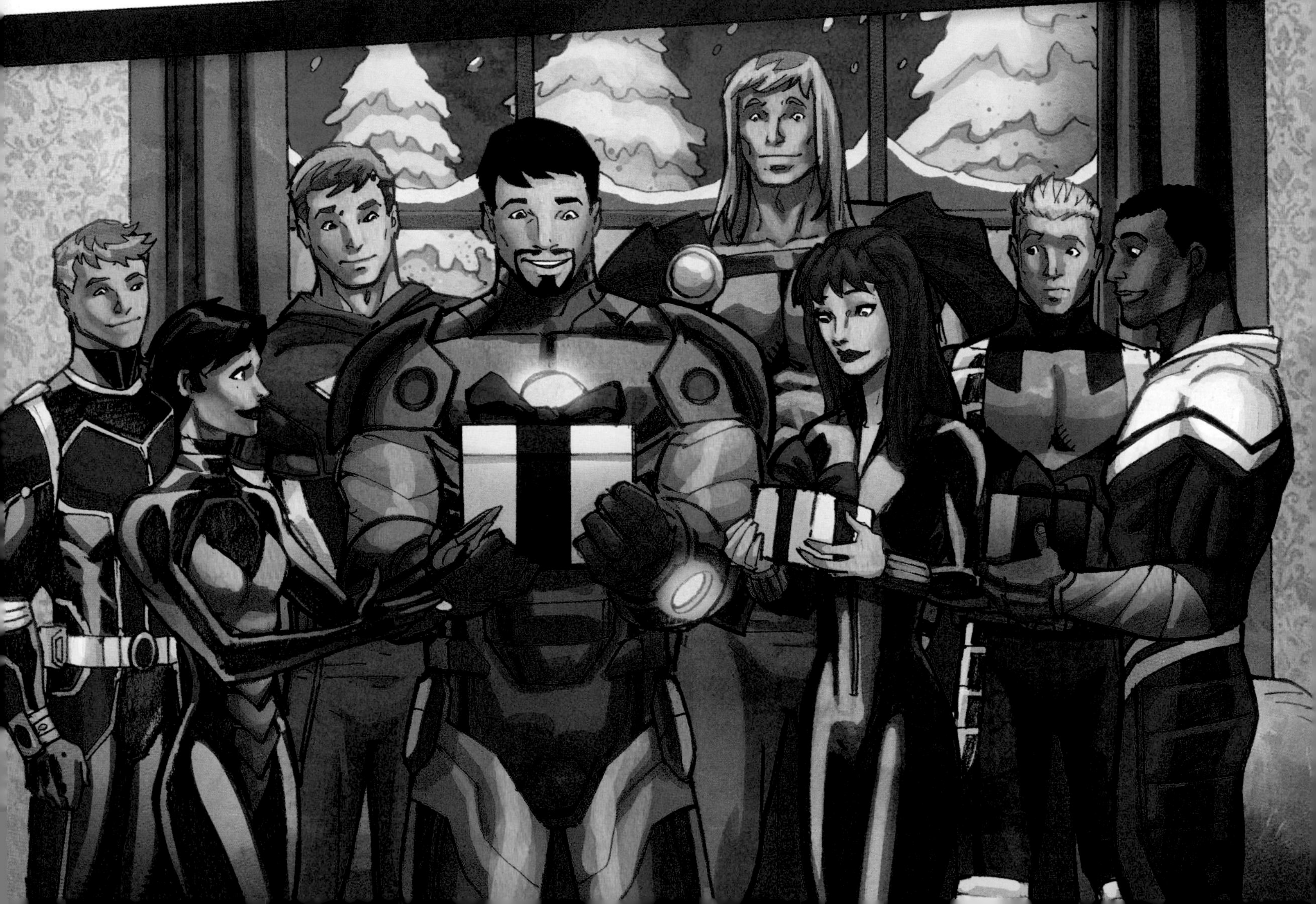

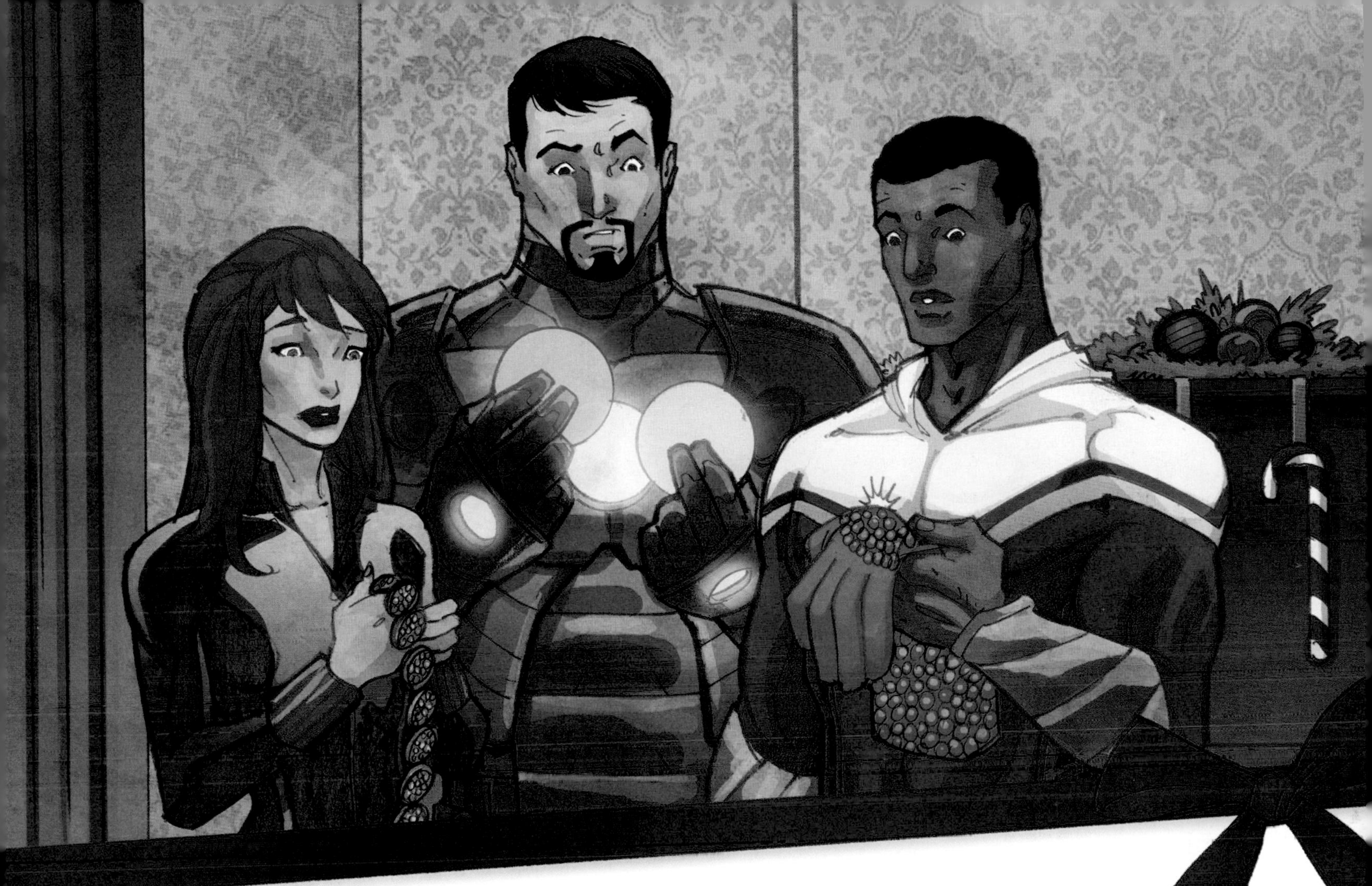

"Oh. A new buckle for my belt. Er, thanks," said Black Widow.

"It's sequined!" Wasp said with enthusiasm.

"A new falconer's glove," Falcon said.

"It's sequined, too!" Wasp explained.

"And I got some, um. . .What exactly are these?" Iron Man asked, holding up a handful of colored disks.

"They're colored plates so you can coordinate your repulsor disks with your mood!"

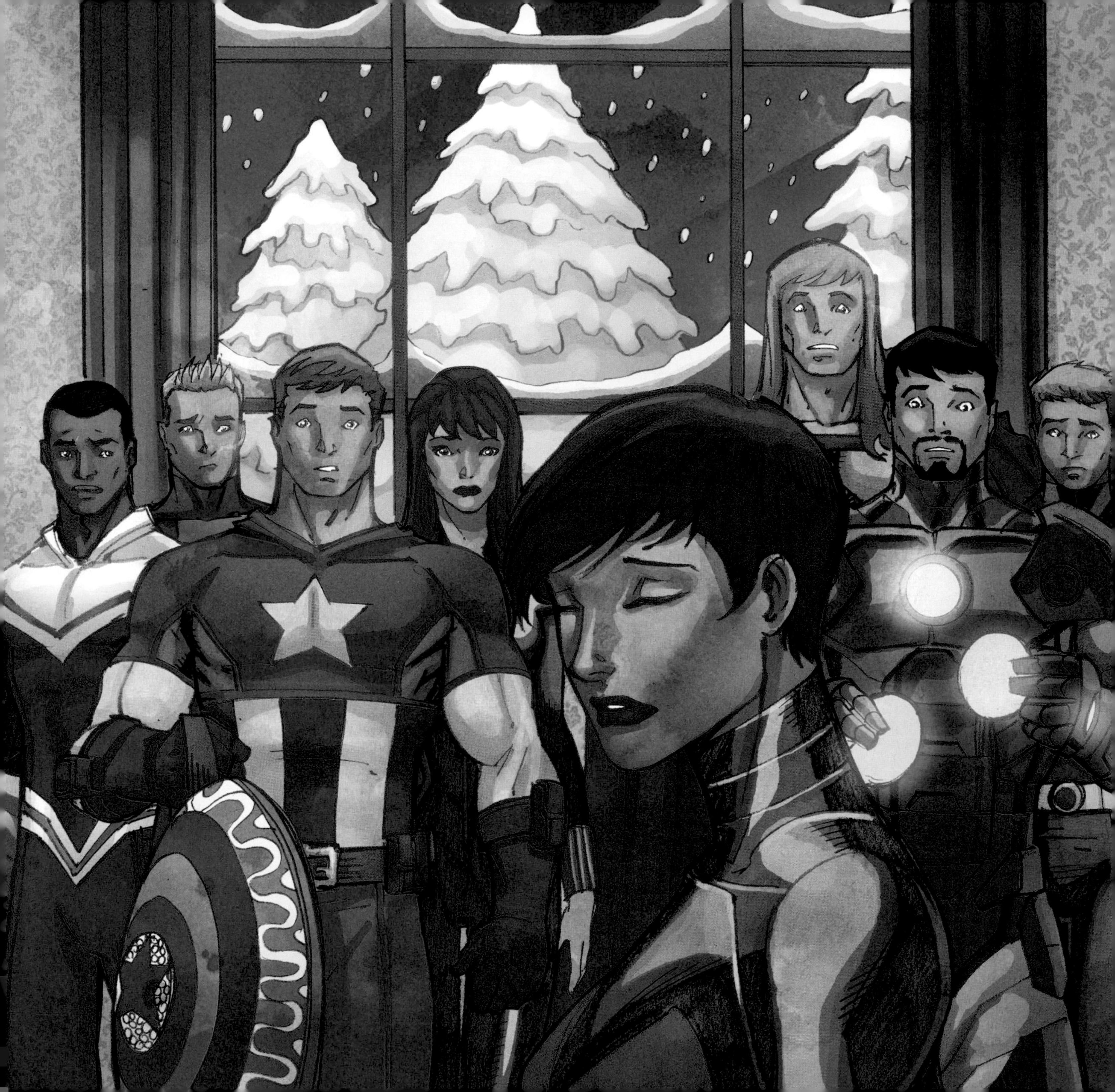

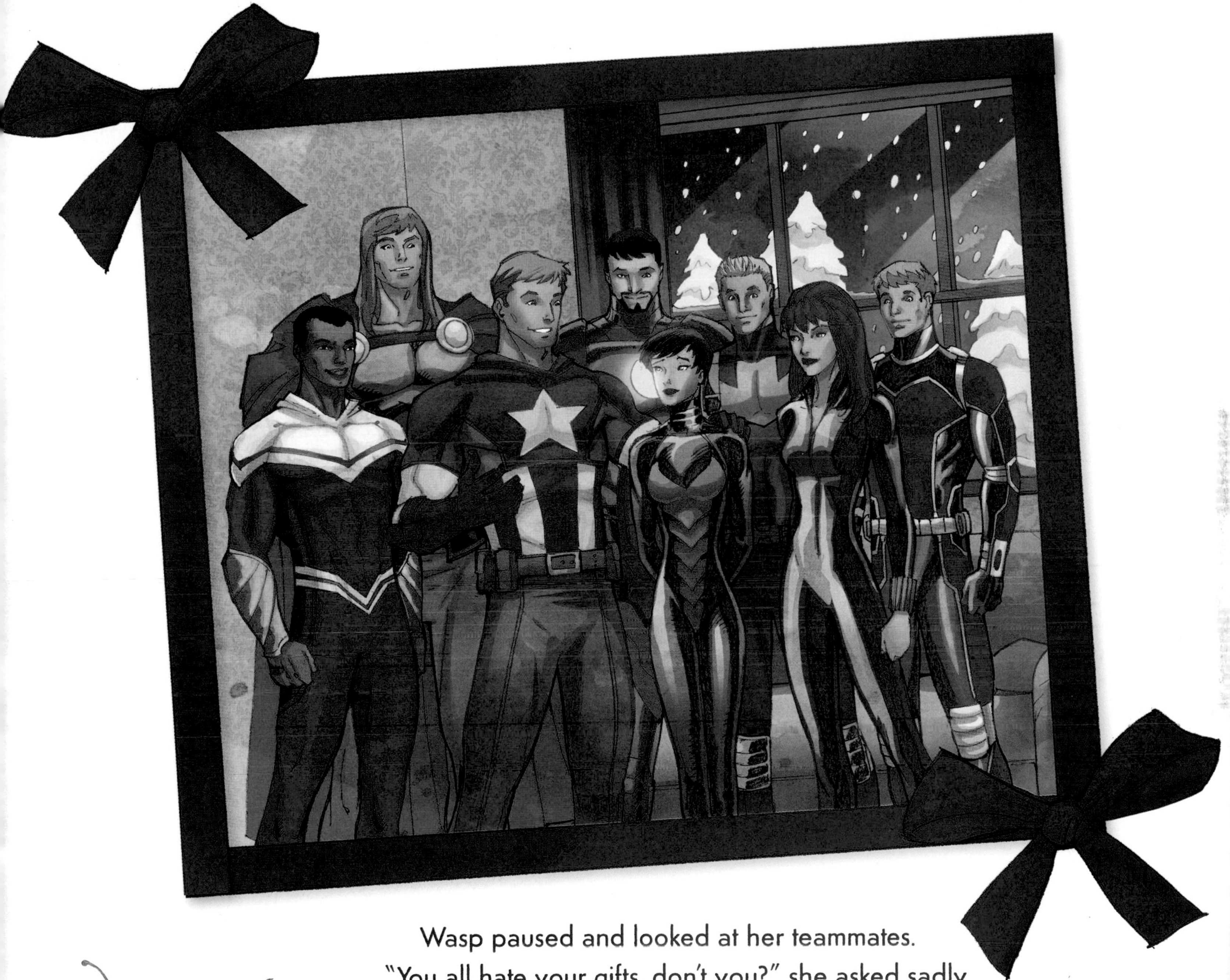

Wasp paused and looked at her teammates. "You all hate your gifts, don't you?" she asked sadly.

"No, no! That's not it at all," Captain America said. "Sorry if you feel hurt, but there's something we have to tell you."

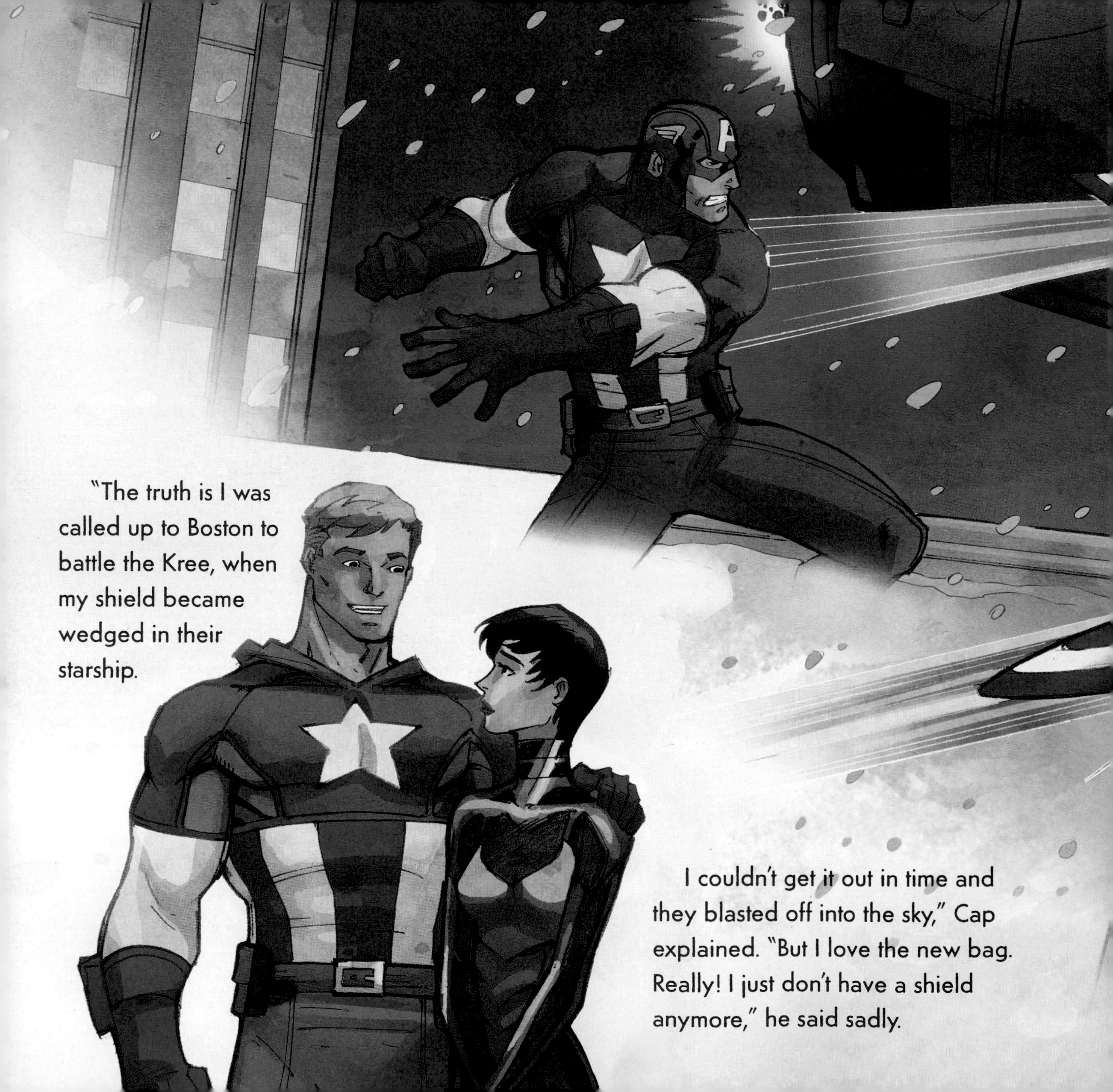

"The truth is I was called up to Boston to battle the Kree, when my shield became wedged in their starship.

I couldn't get it out in time and they blasted off into the sky," Cap explained. "But I love the new bag. Really! I just don't have a shield anymore," he said sadly.

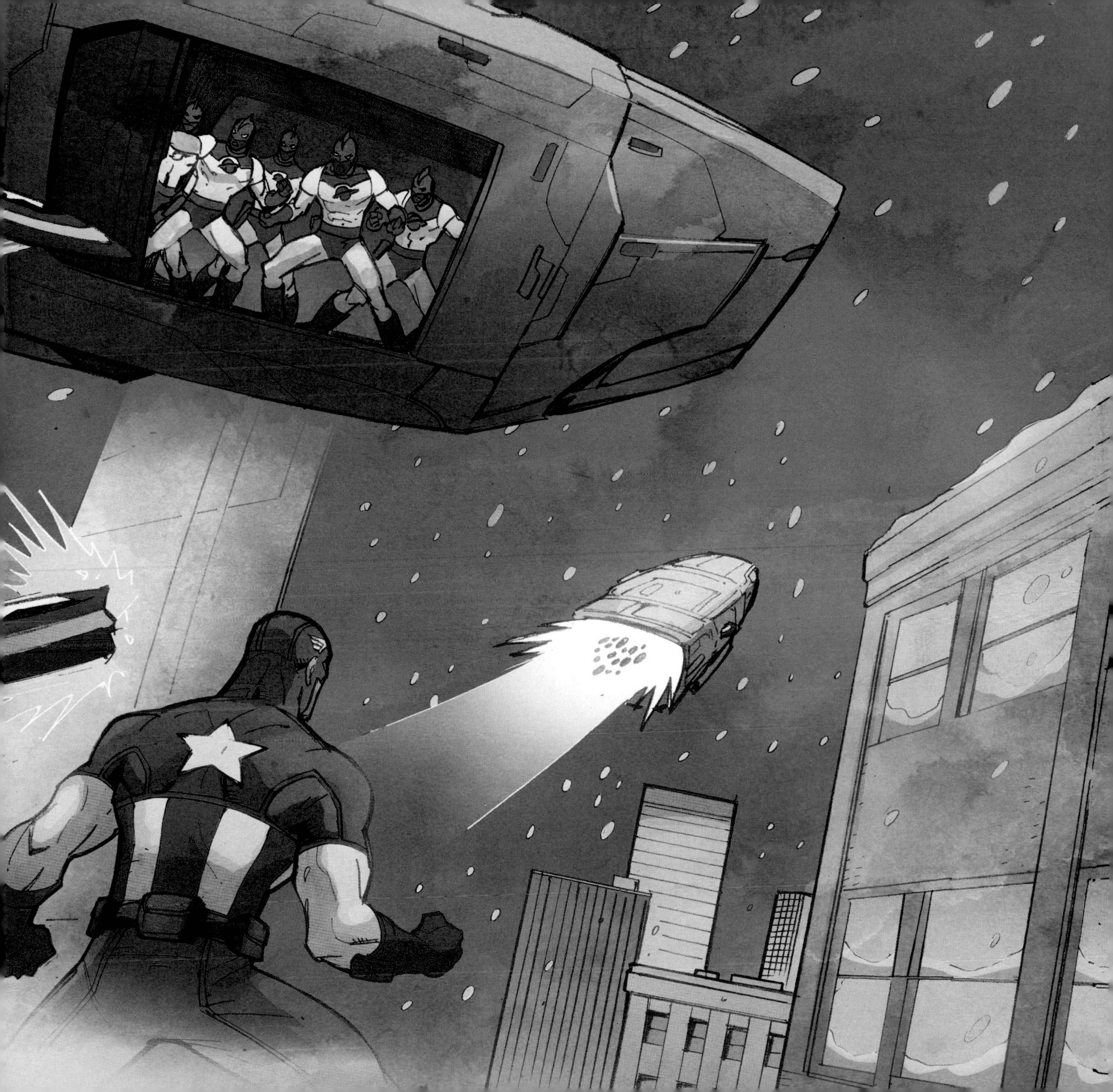

"And mine mighty helmet was swept away whilst I battled Loki this morning," Thor confessed. "Thus why I was saddened when I received thy gift of wings."

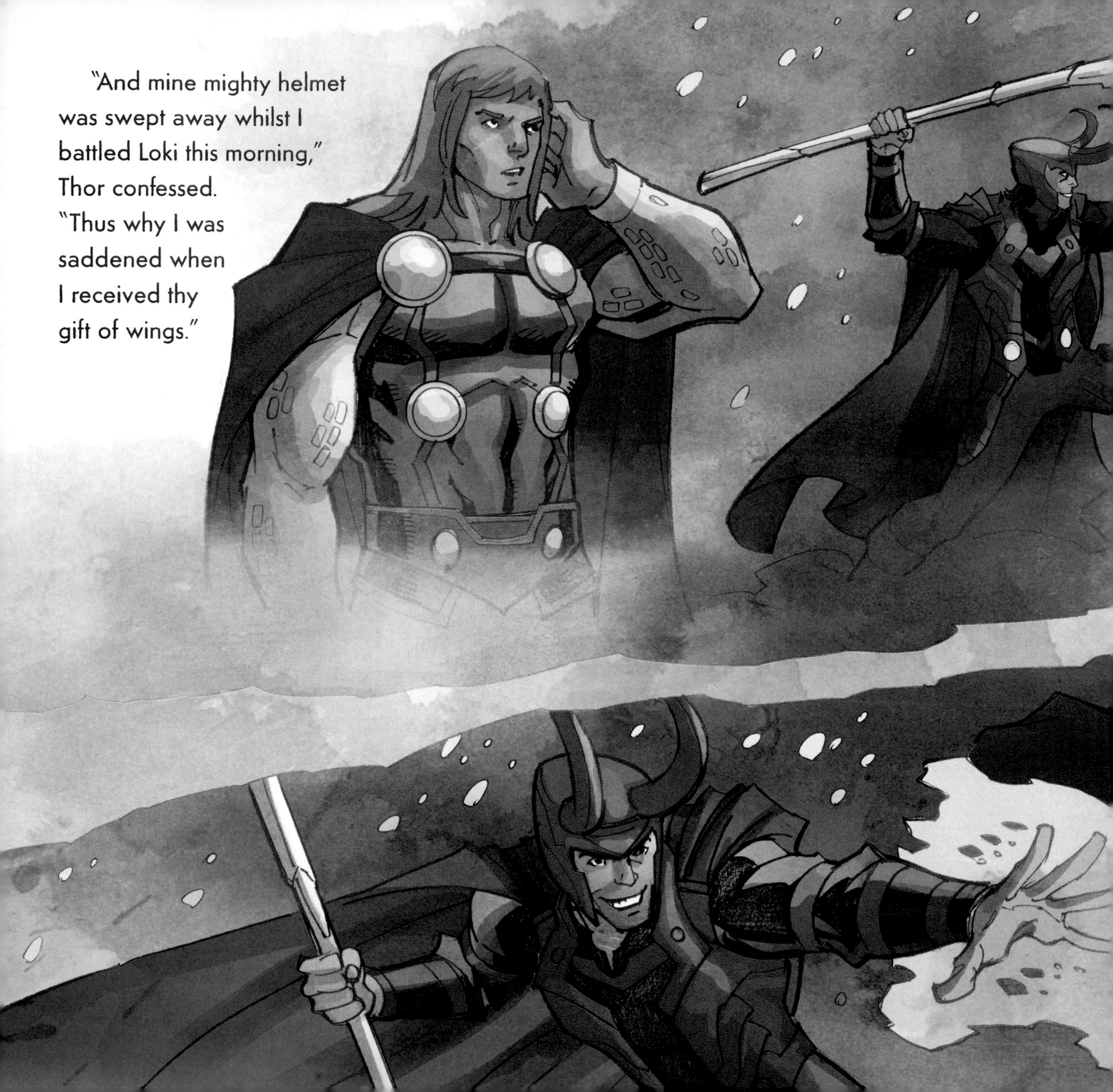

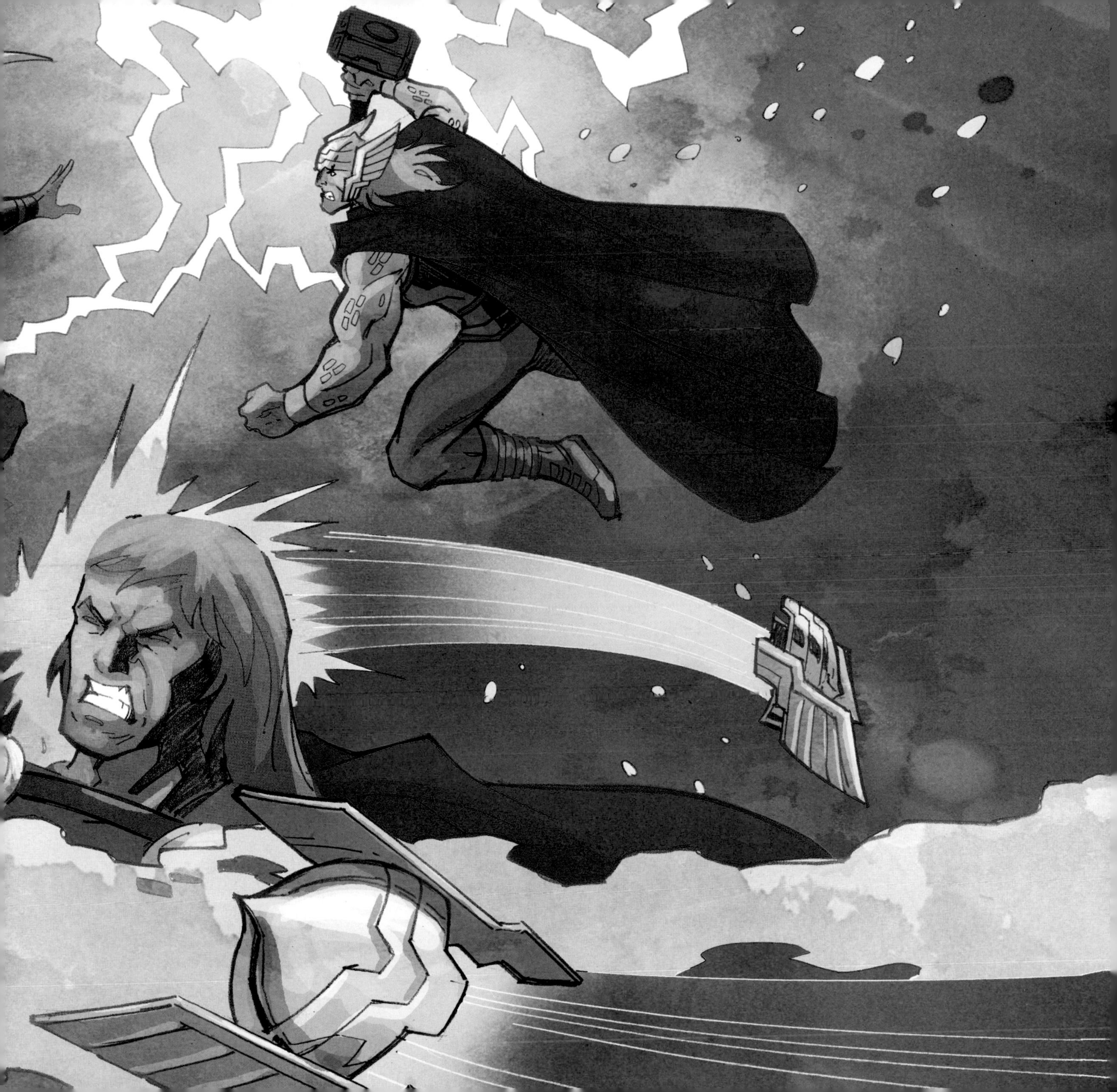

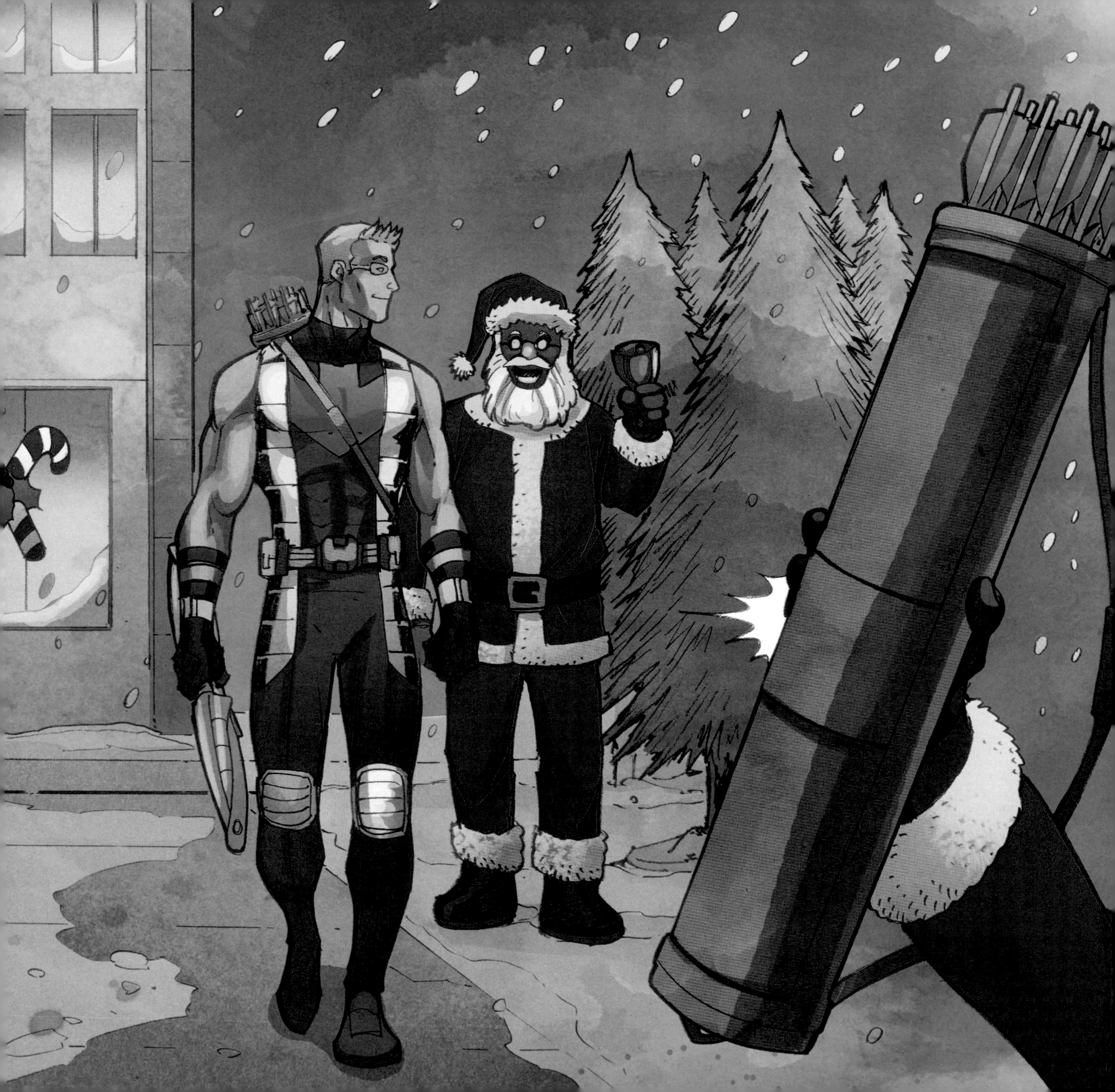

“And my bag that was full of arrows was swiped by a Skrull pretending to be Santa outside Rockefeller Center,” Hawkeye admitted.

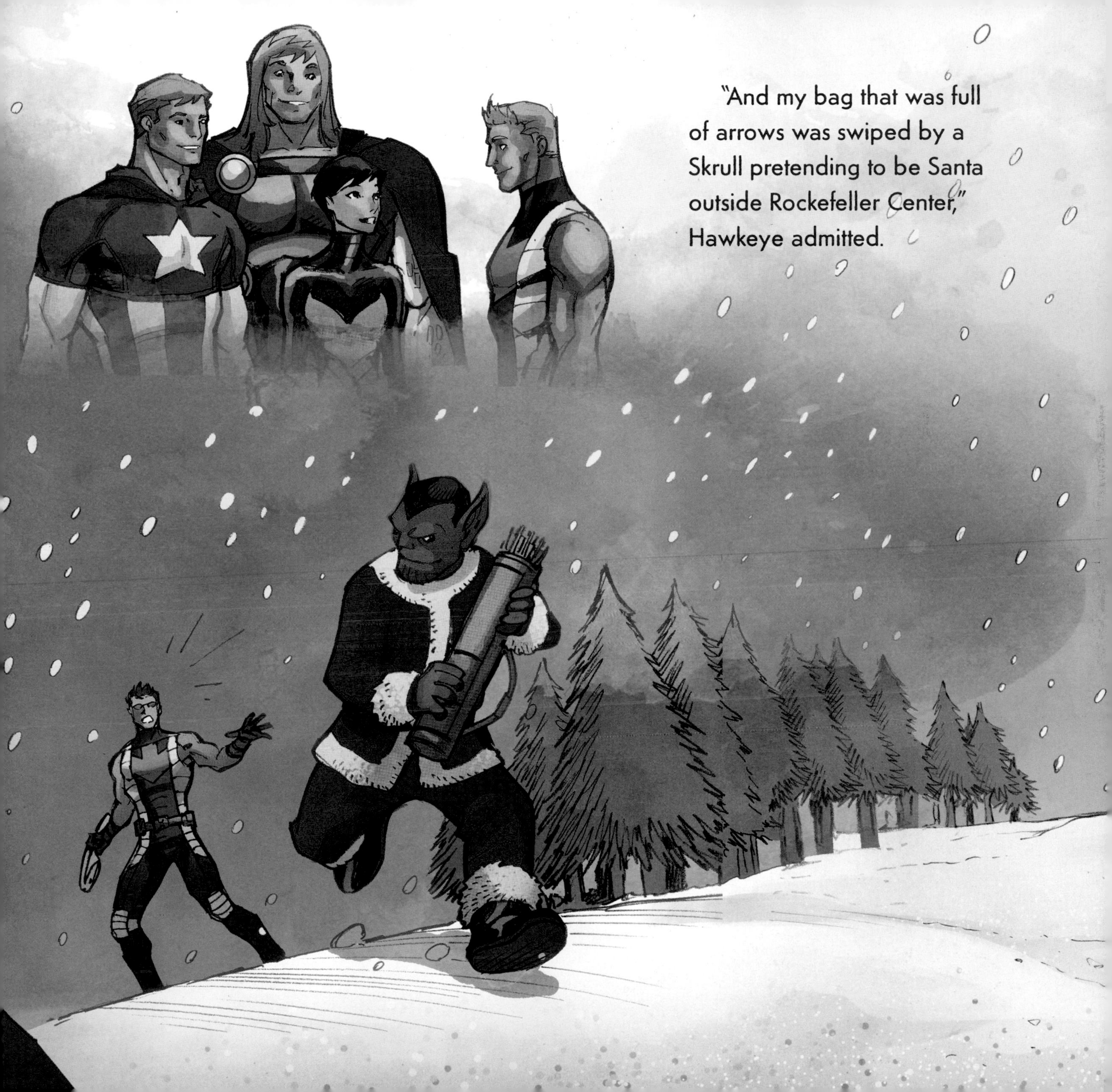

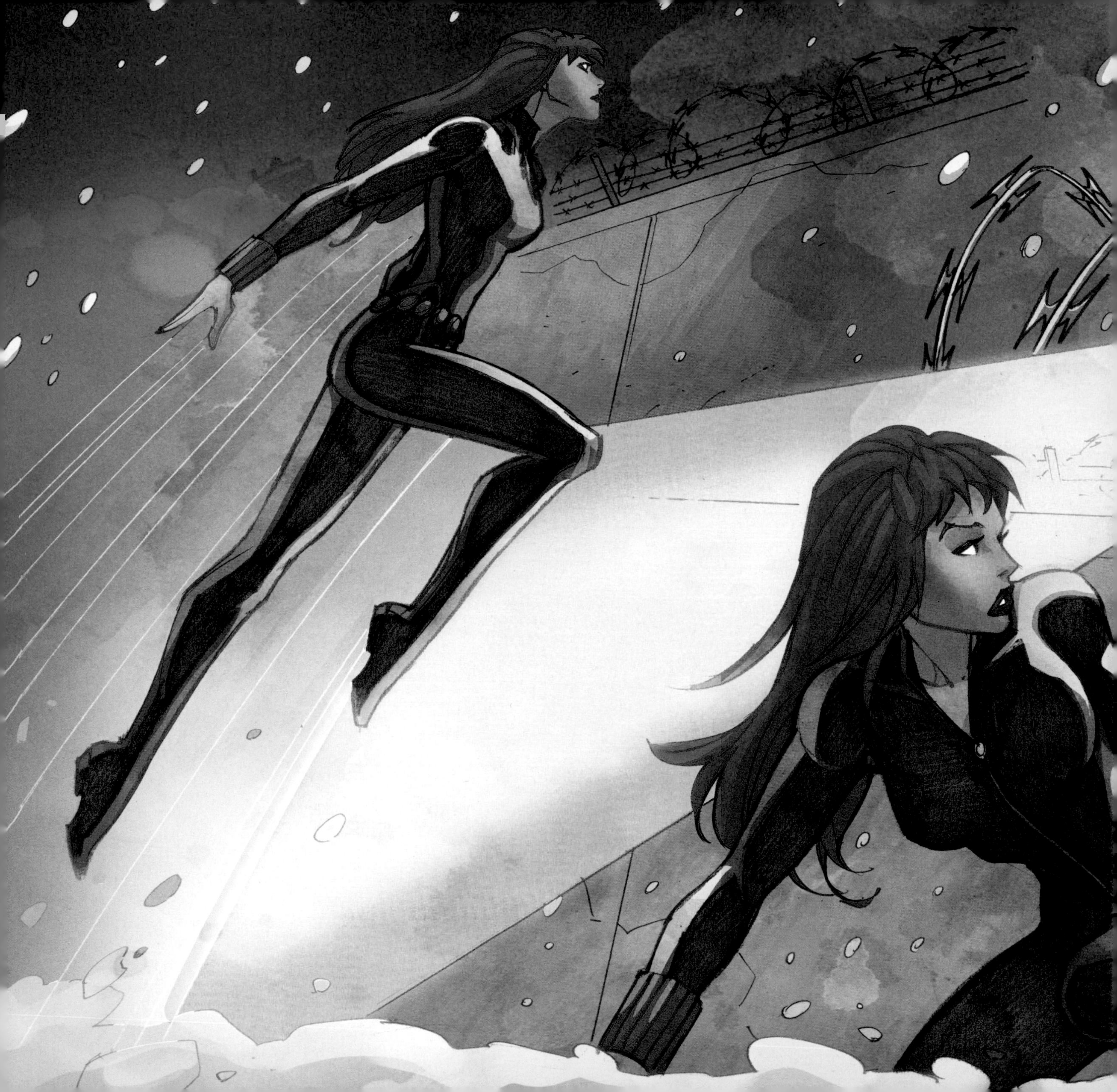

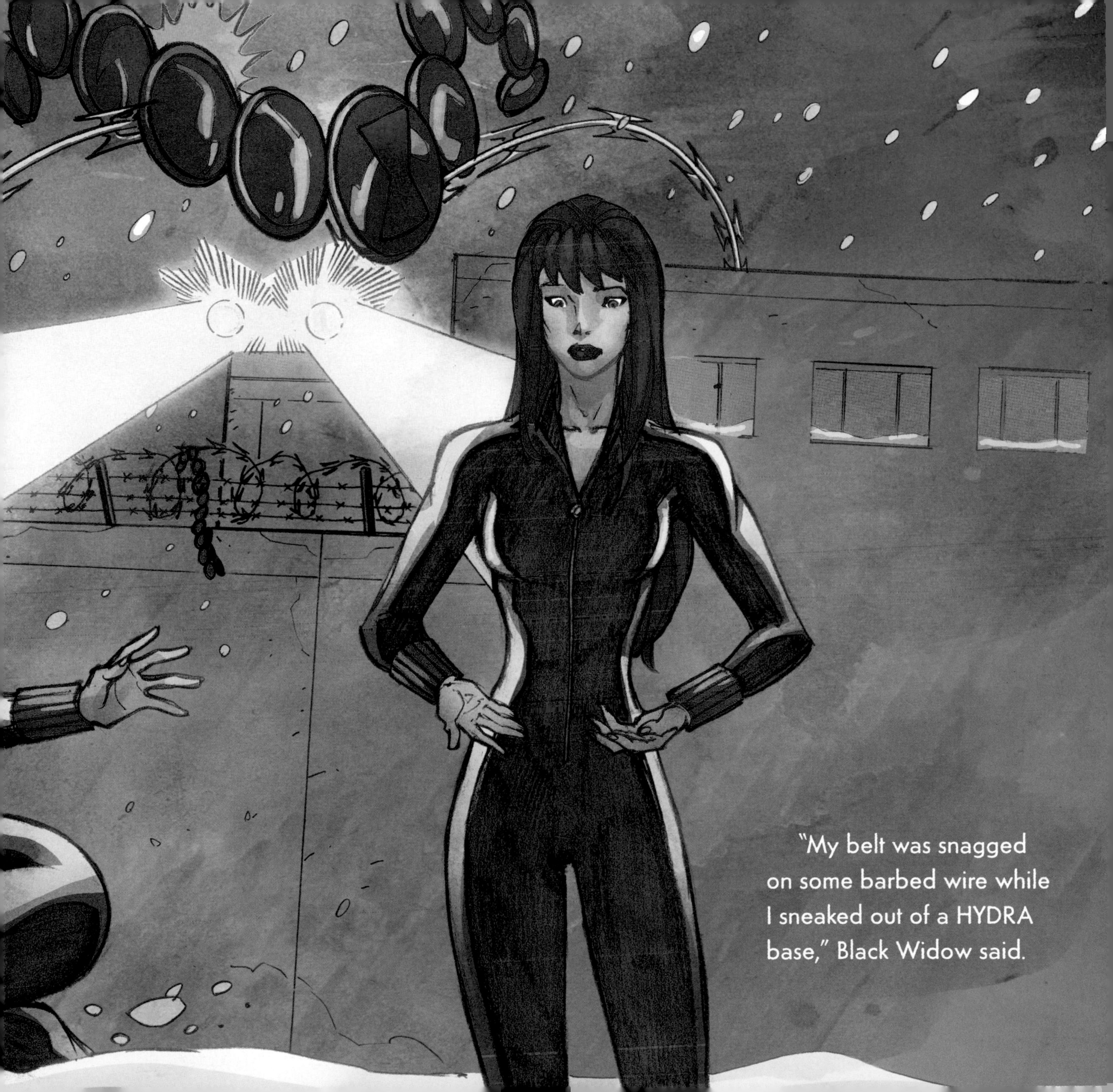

"My belt was snagged on some barbed wire while I sneaked out of a HYDRA base," Black Widow said.

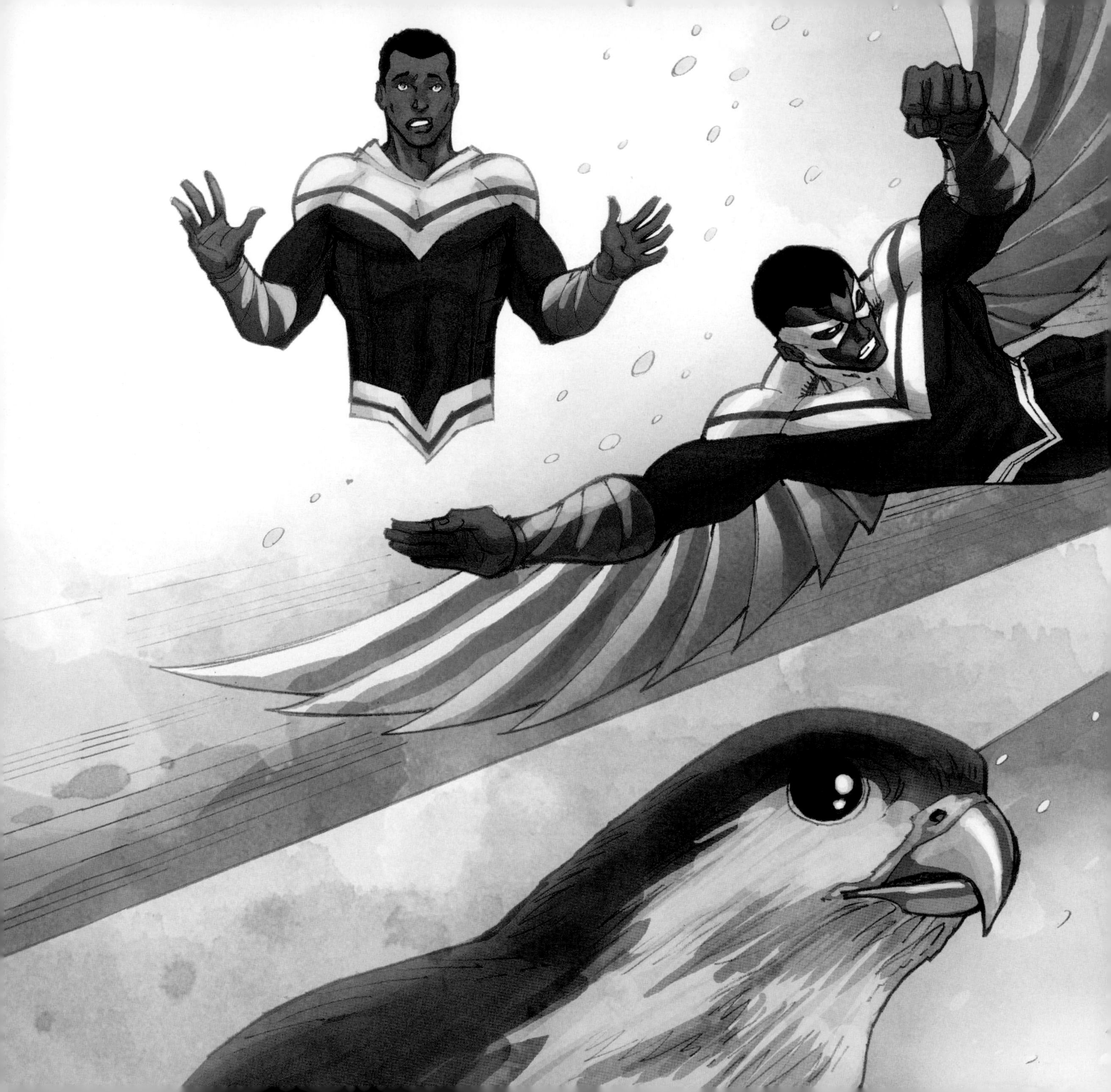

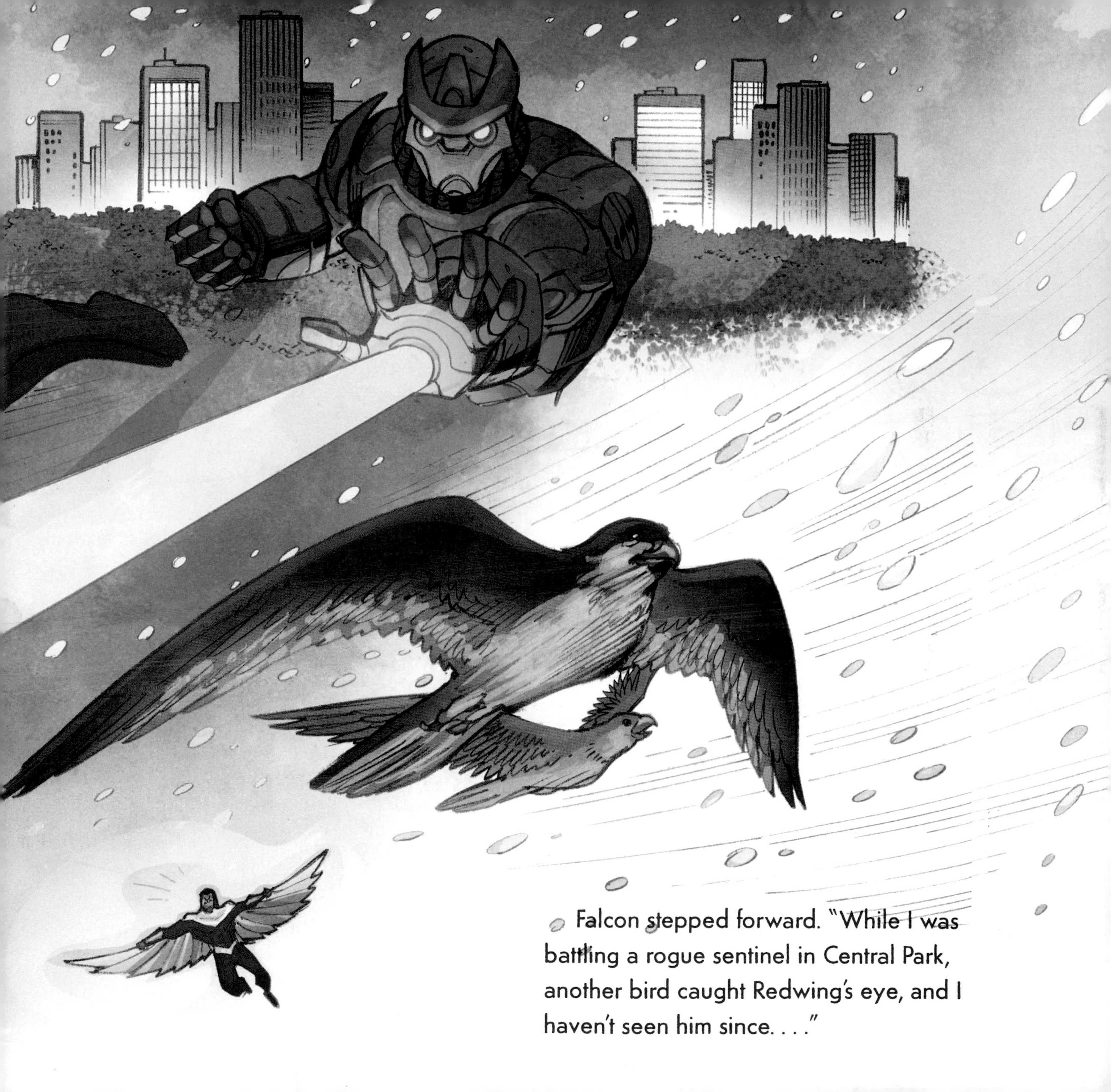

Falcon stepped forward. "While I was battling a rogue sentinel in Central Park, another bird caught Redwing's eye, and I haven't seen him since. . . ."

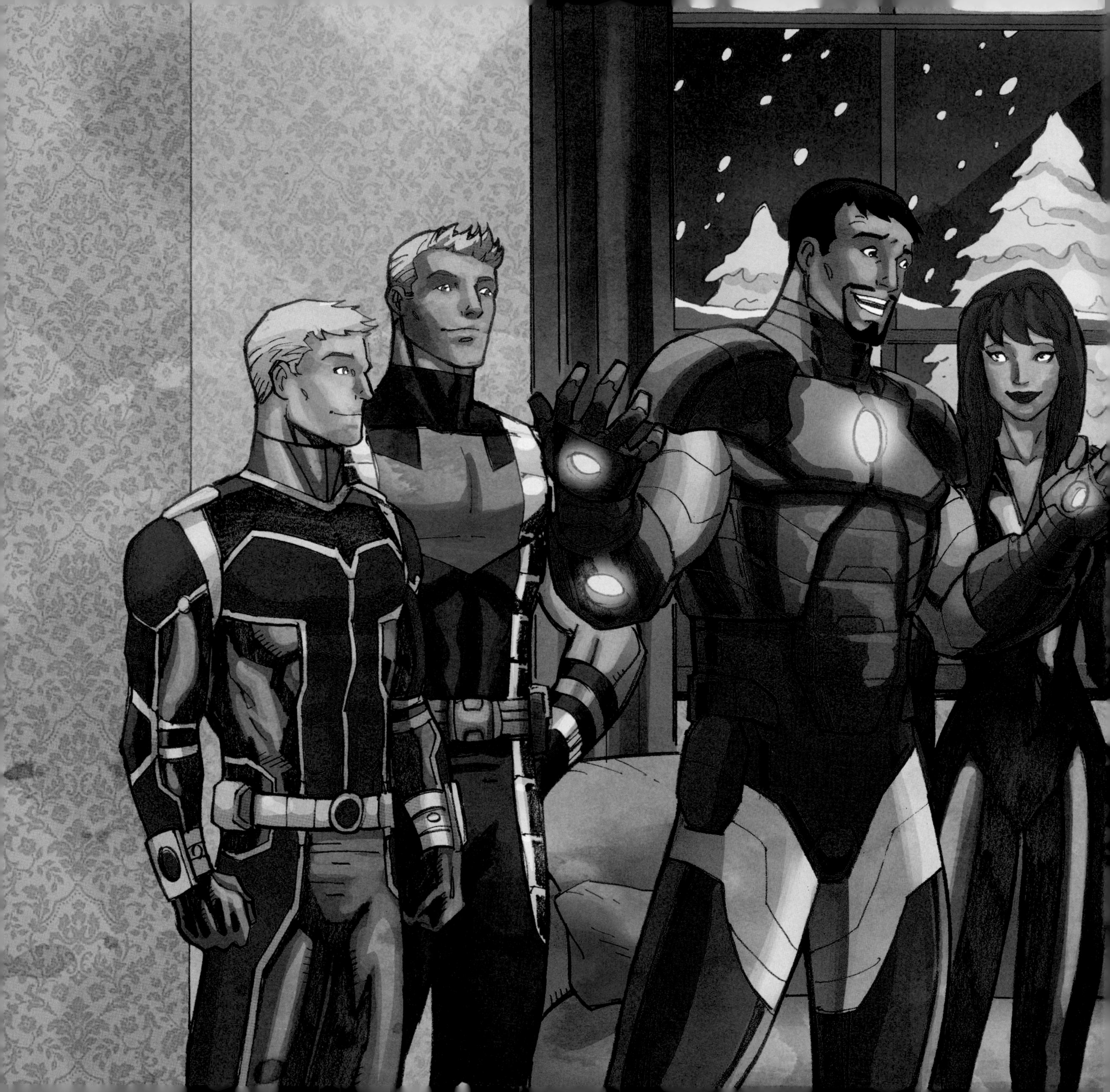

"I didn't lose anything," Iron Man said with a shrug. "I just think your gift is a little weird."

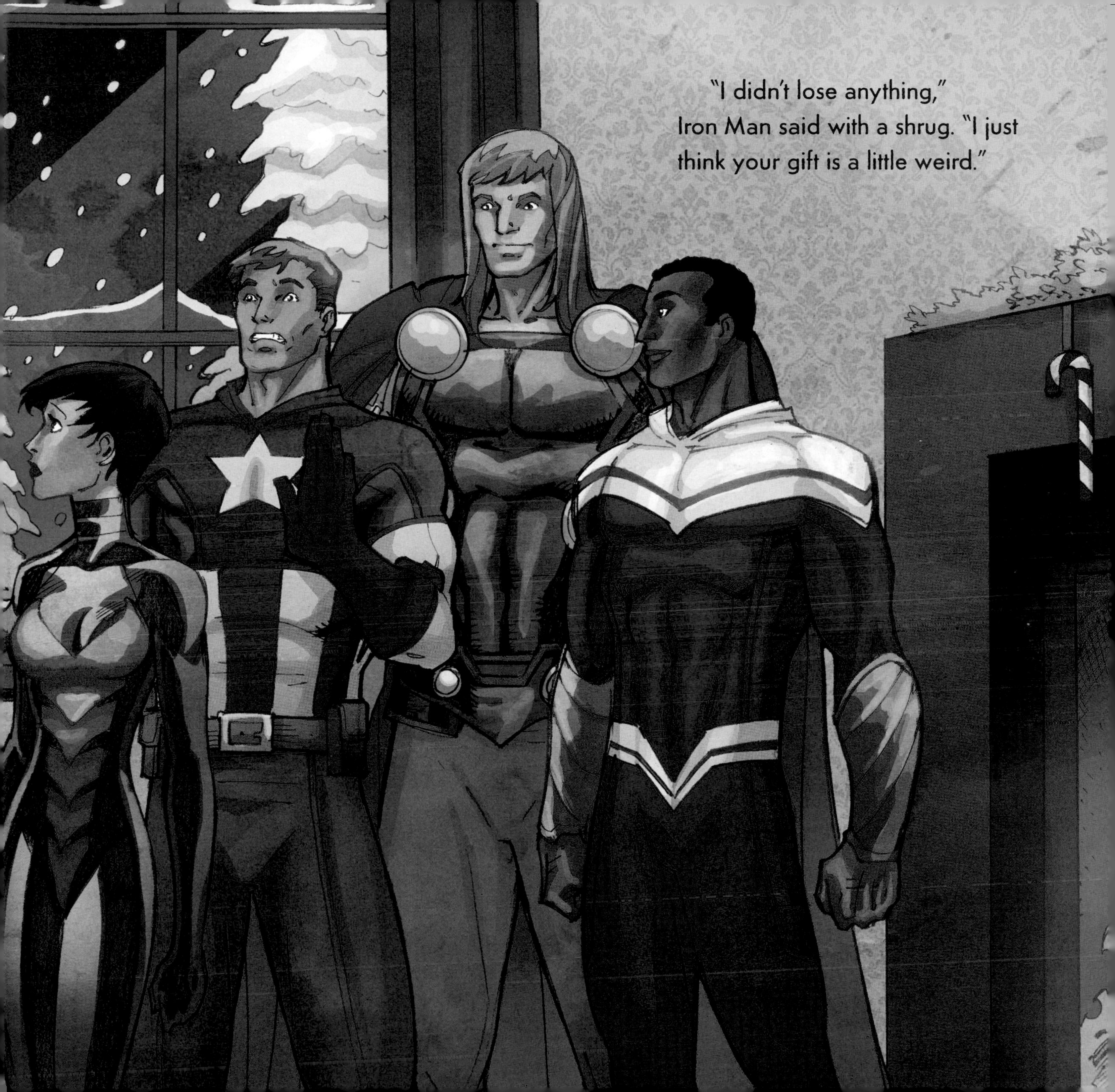

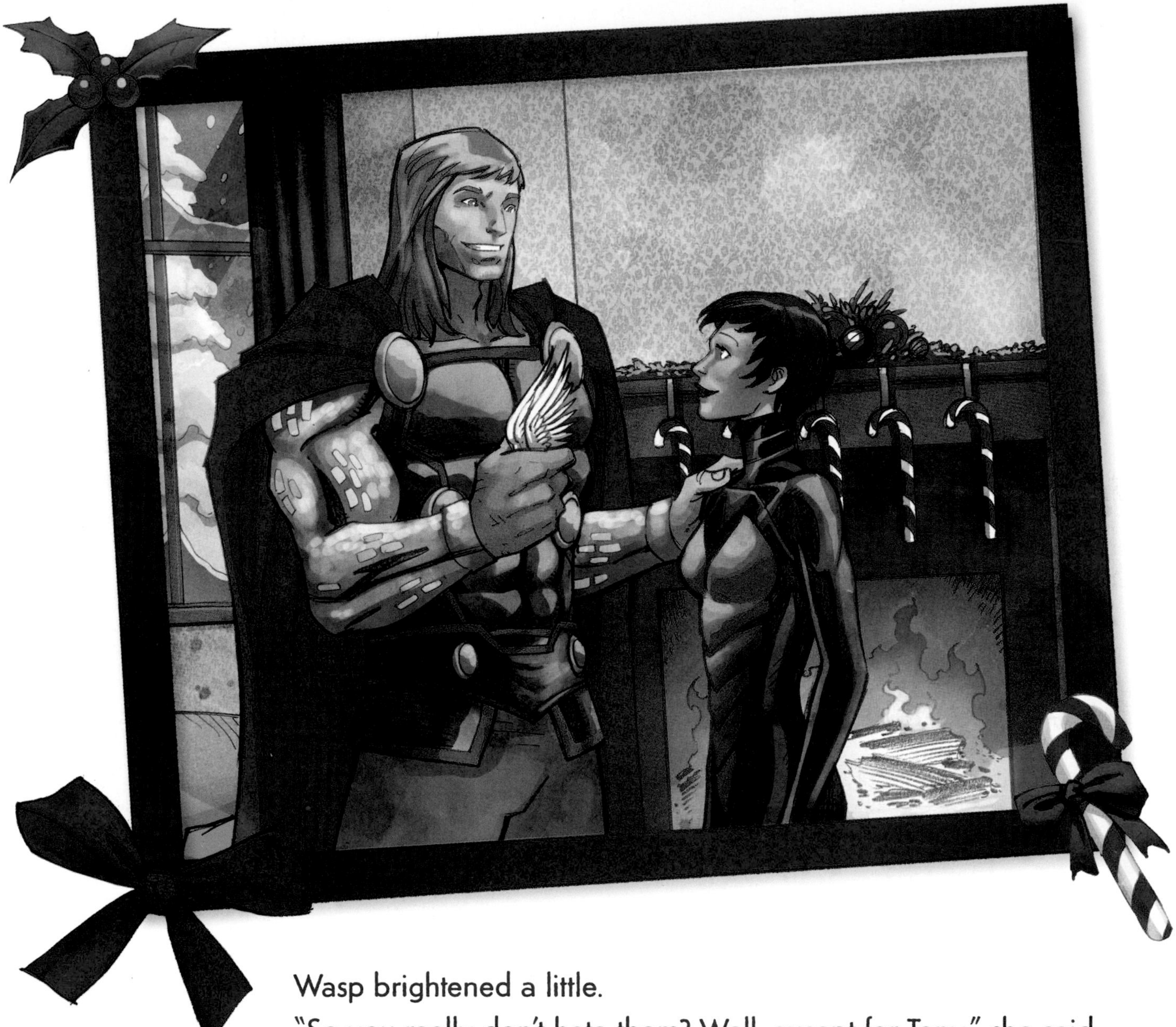

Wasp brightened a little.

"So you really don't hate them? Well, except for Tony," she said, sneering lightheartedly at Iron Man.

"If my helmet were here right now I would proudly affix these wings to its flanks," Thor said, placing a reassuring hand on Wasp's shoulder.

Wasp smiled. "Thanks, Thor."

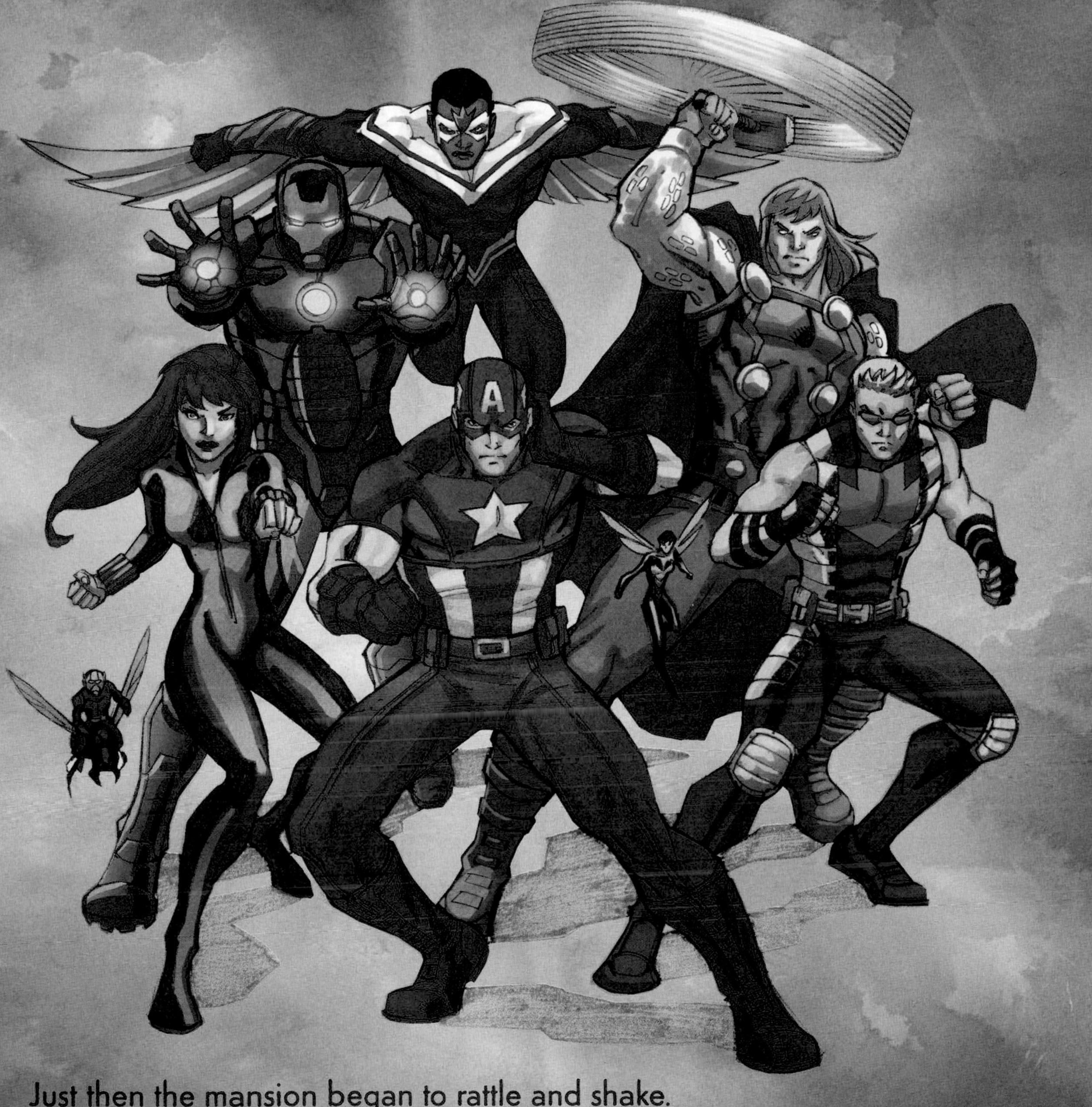

Just then the mansion began to rattle and shake.

"We're under attack!" Iron Man cried. "Don't Super Villains have the night off? I mean, it *is* the holidays!"

"Evil never rests, and neither do the Avengers," Captain America said proudly, clenching his fist and preparing for battle.

But as the threat crashed through the wall, spraying bricks everywhere, the Avengers realized it wasn't a villain at all.

"Happy holidays. . .from HULK!"

The Green Goliath had made it home for the festive winter's night, after all. And he'd brought presents!

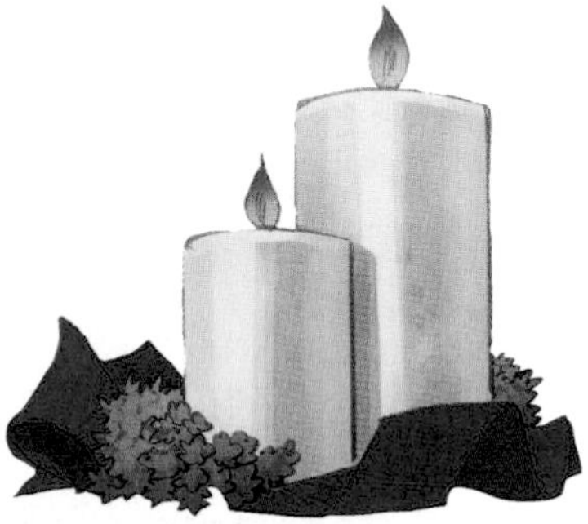

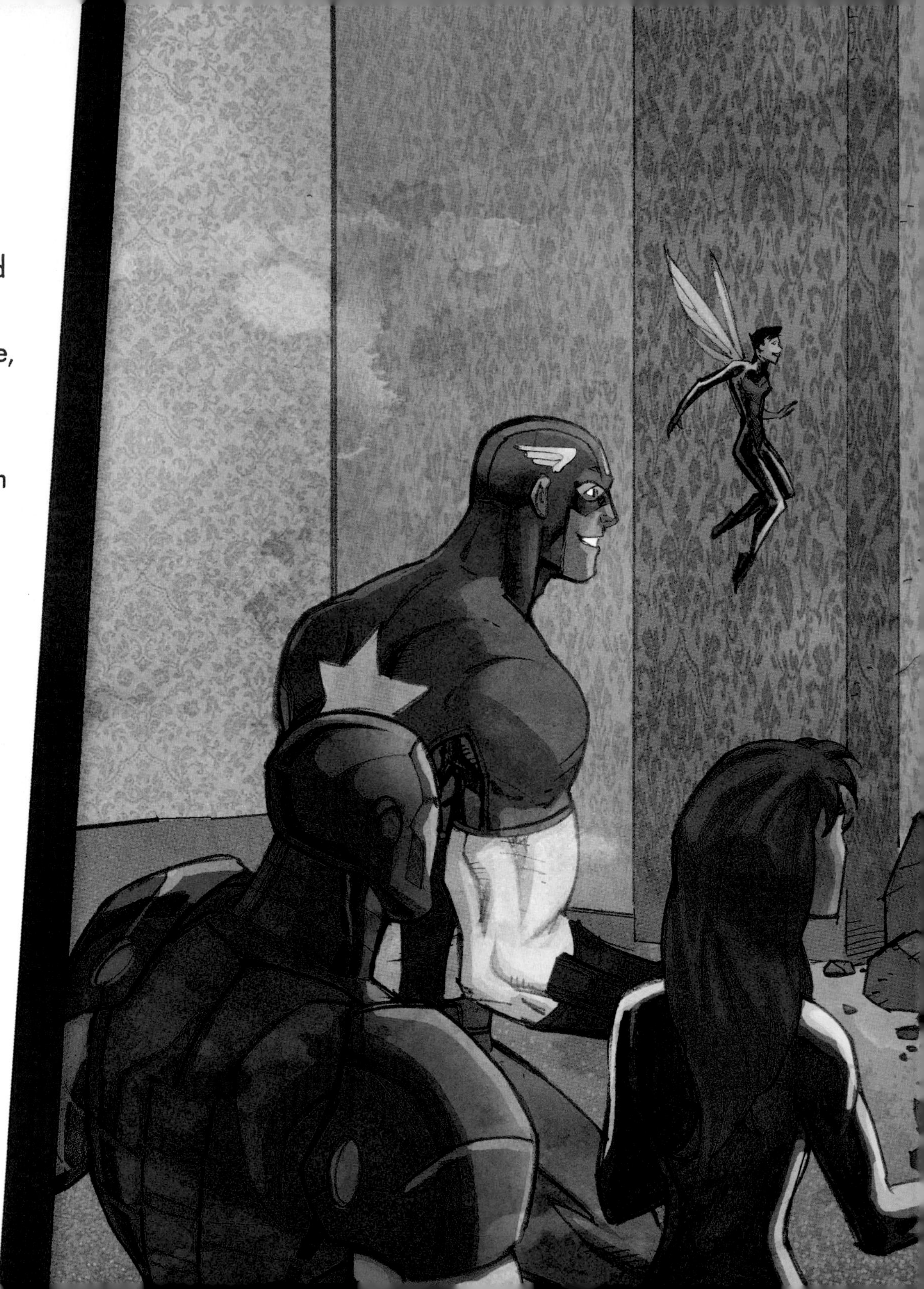

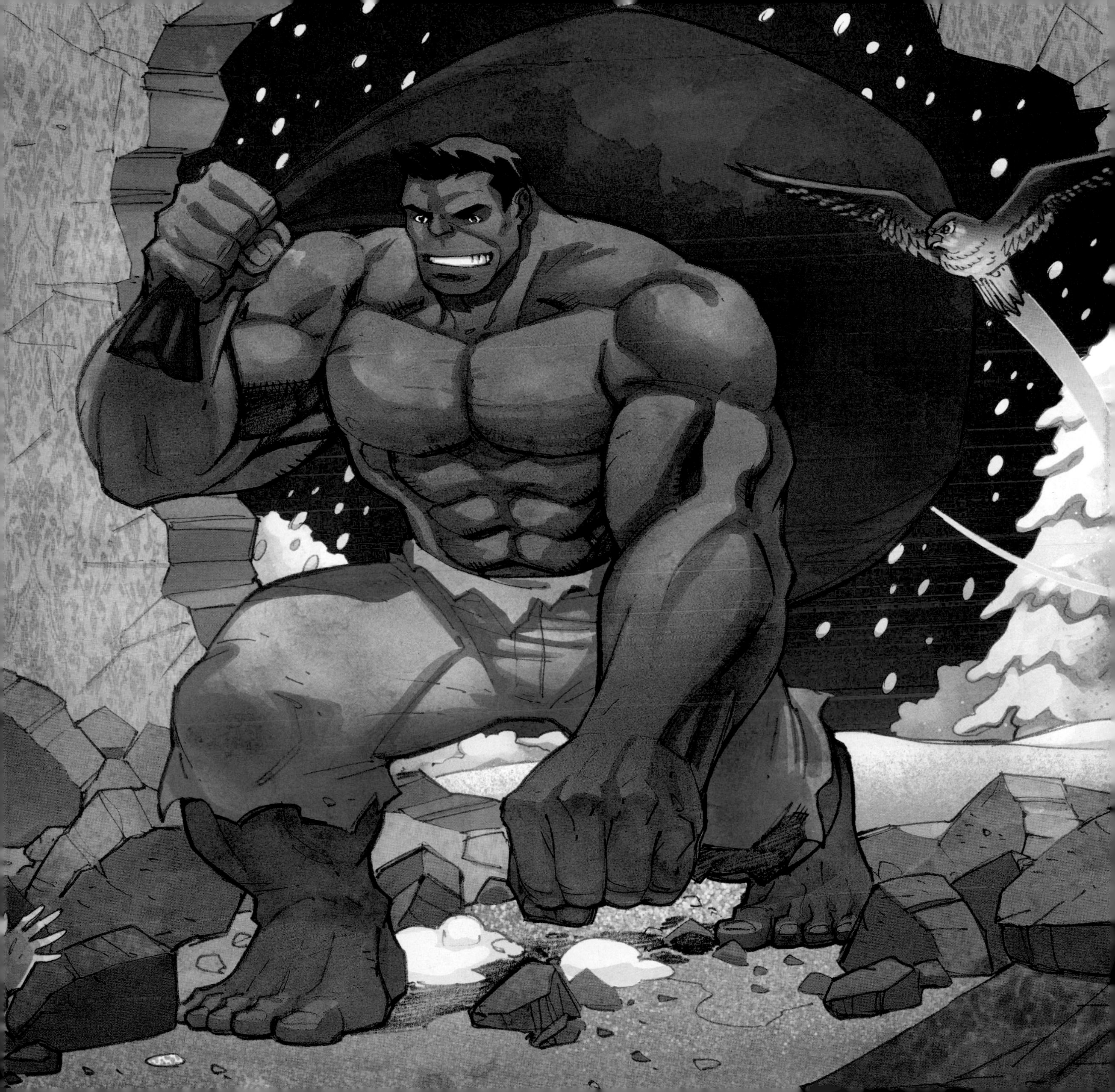

"HULK out of gift ideas. But HULK find things he thinks Avengers will like."

The Hulk opened the huge bag he was carrying and presented his gifts—Cap's shield, Thor's helmet, Black Widow's belt, Hawkeye's quiver pack, and more!

"Hulk, how did you. . . ?" the Wasp asked.

"Let's just say Hulk very busy smashing all day long. Now HULK relax and enjoy holiday with friends!"

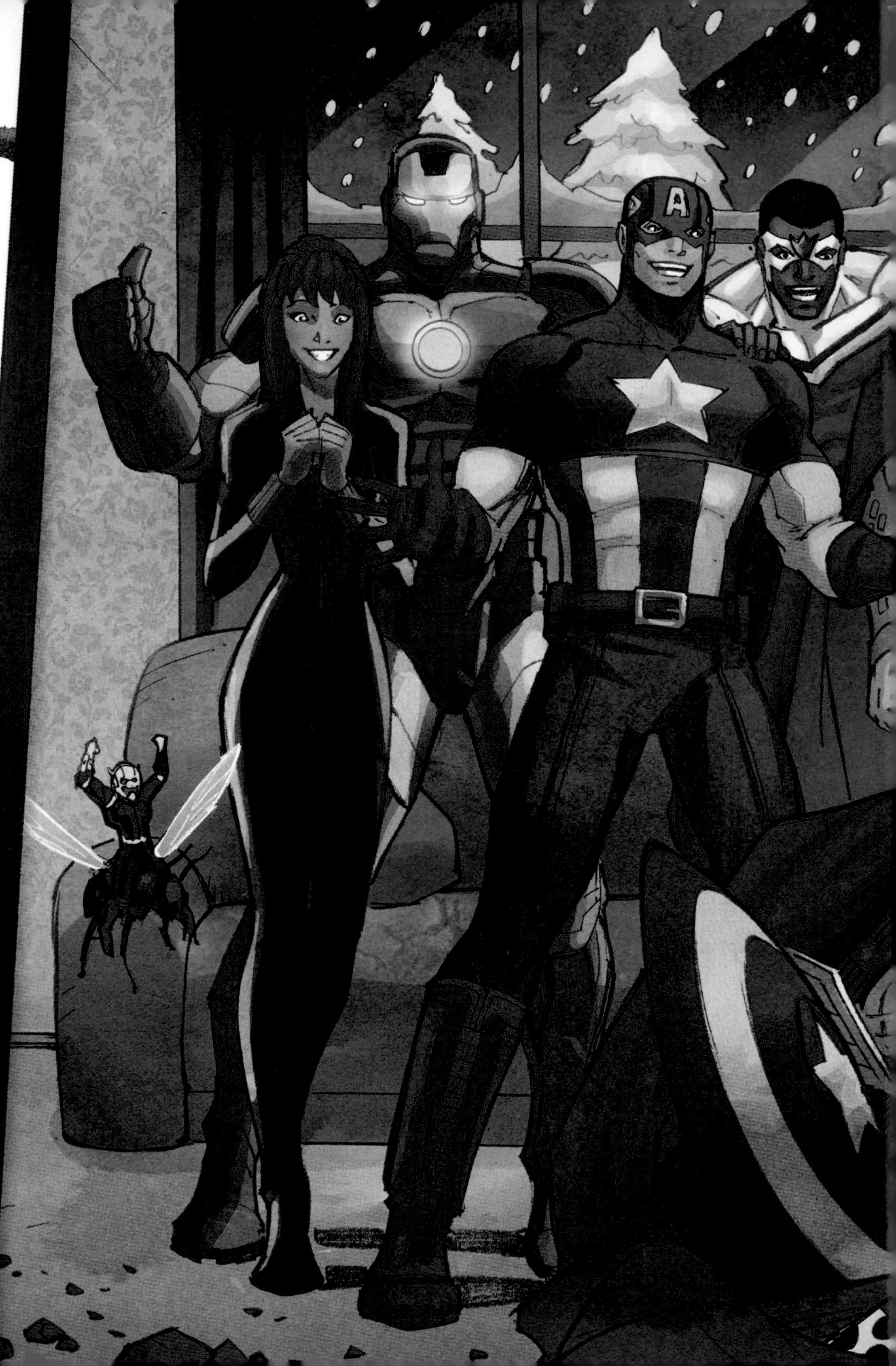

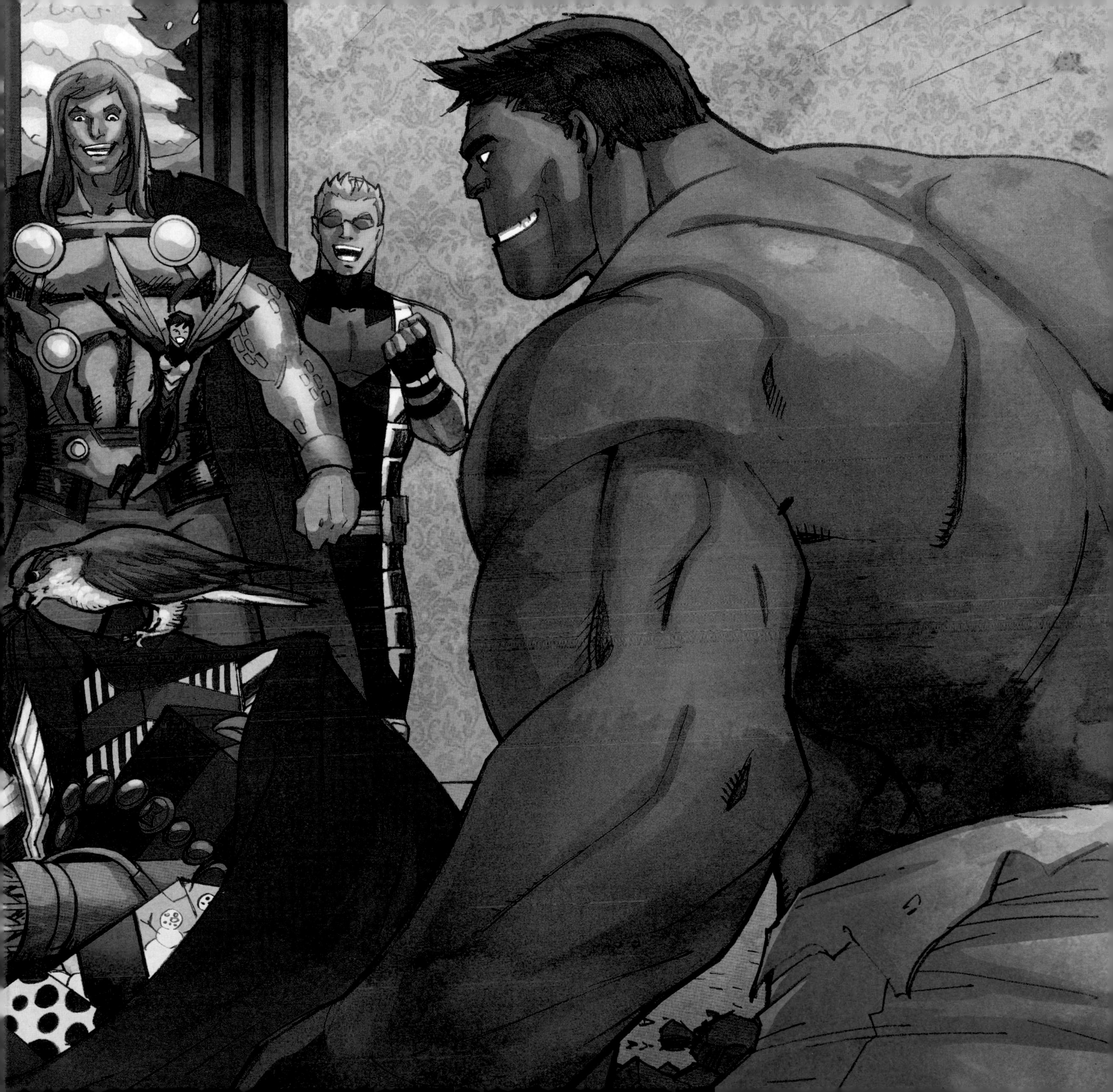

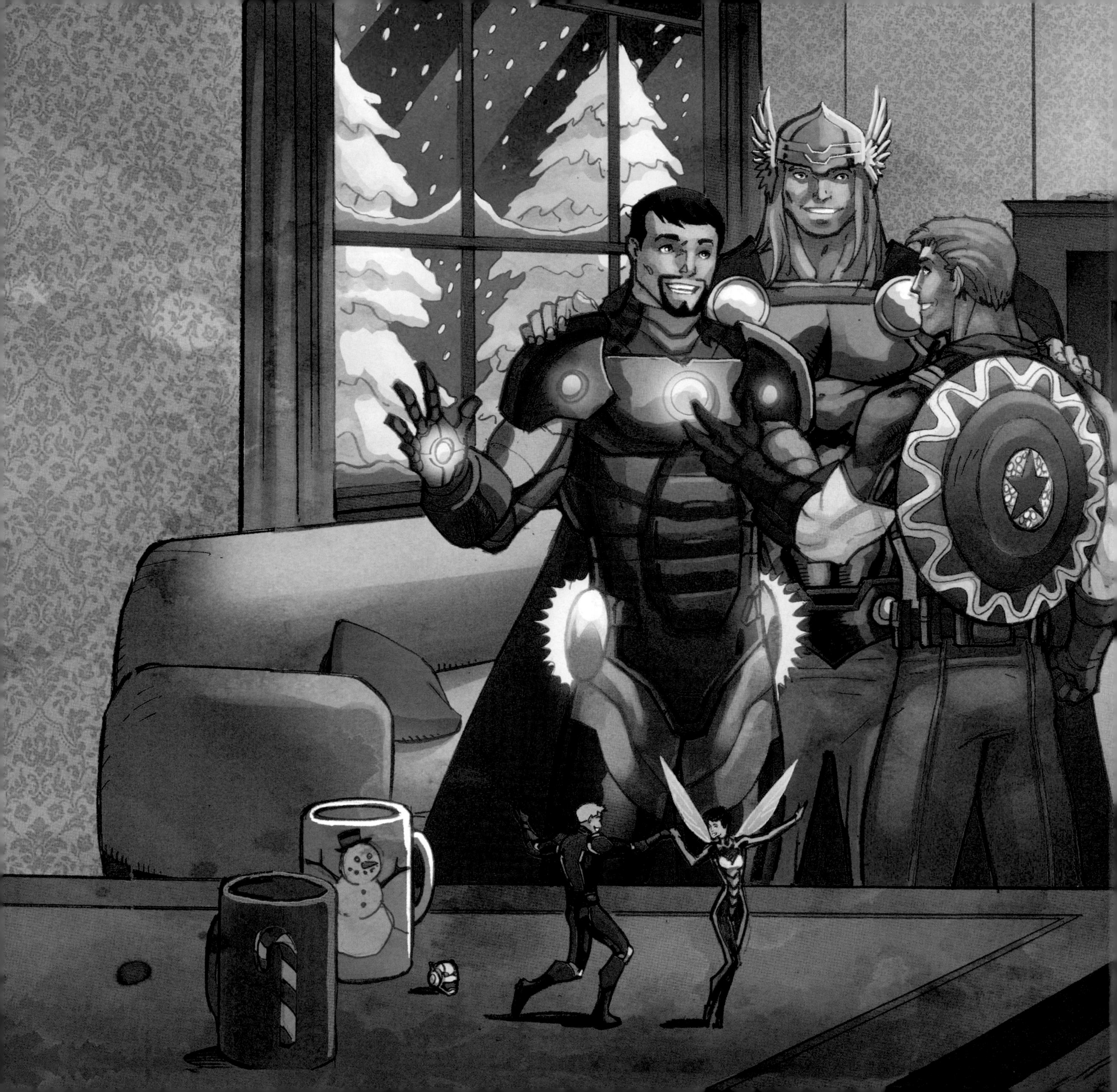

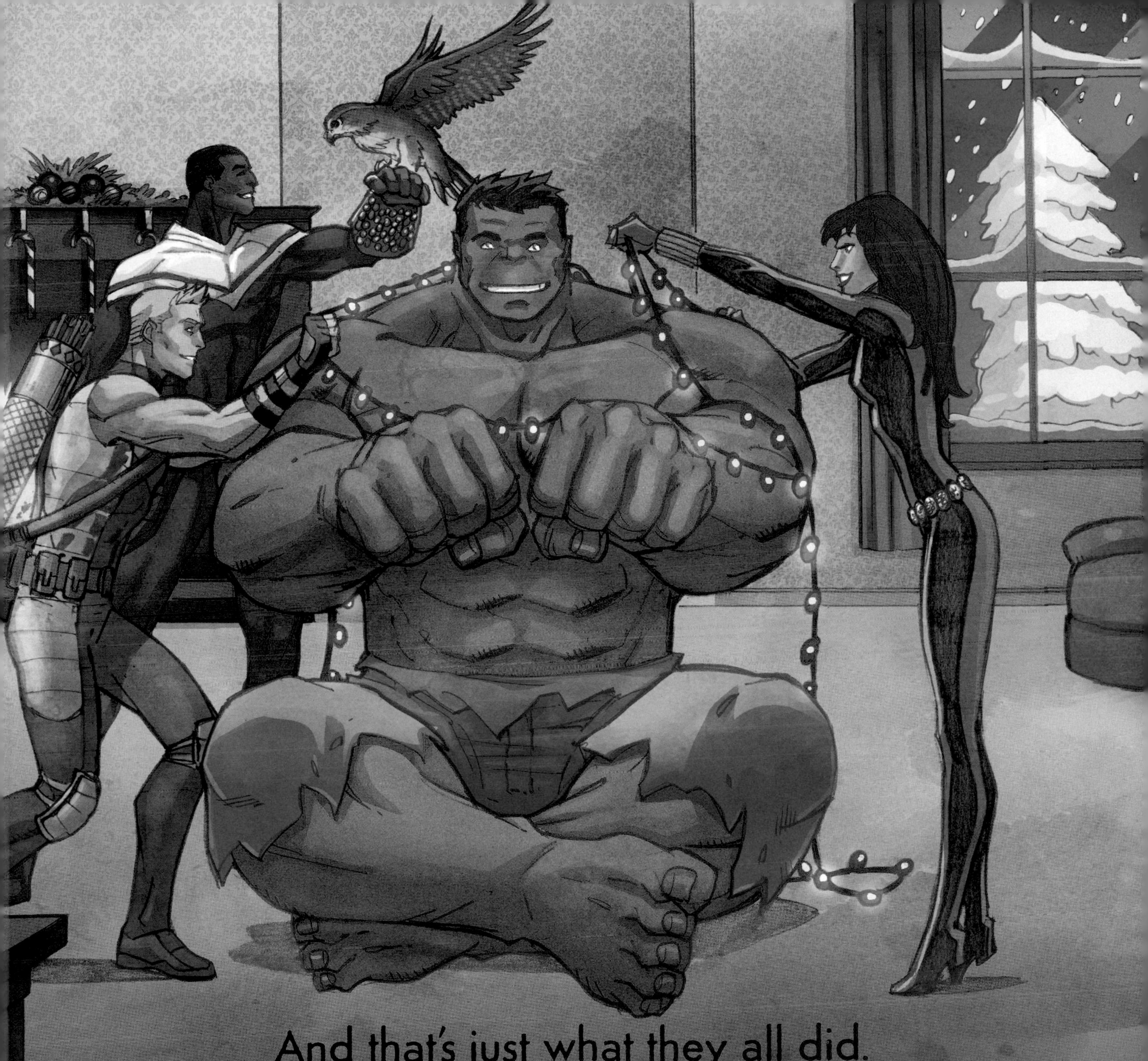

And that's just what they all did.

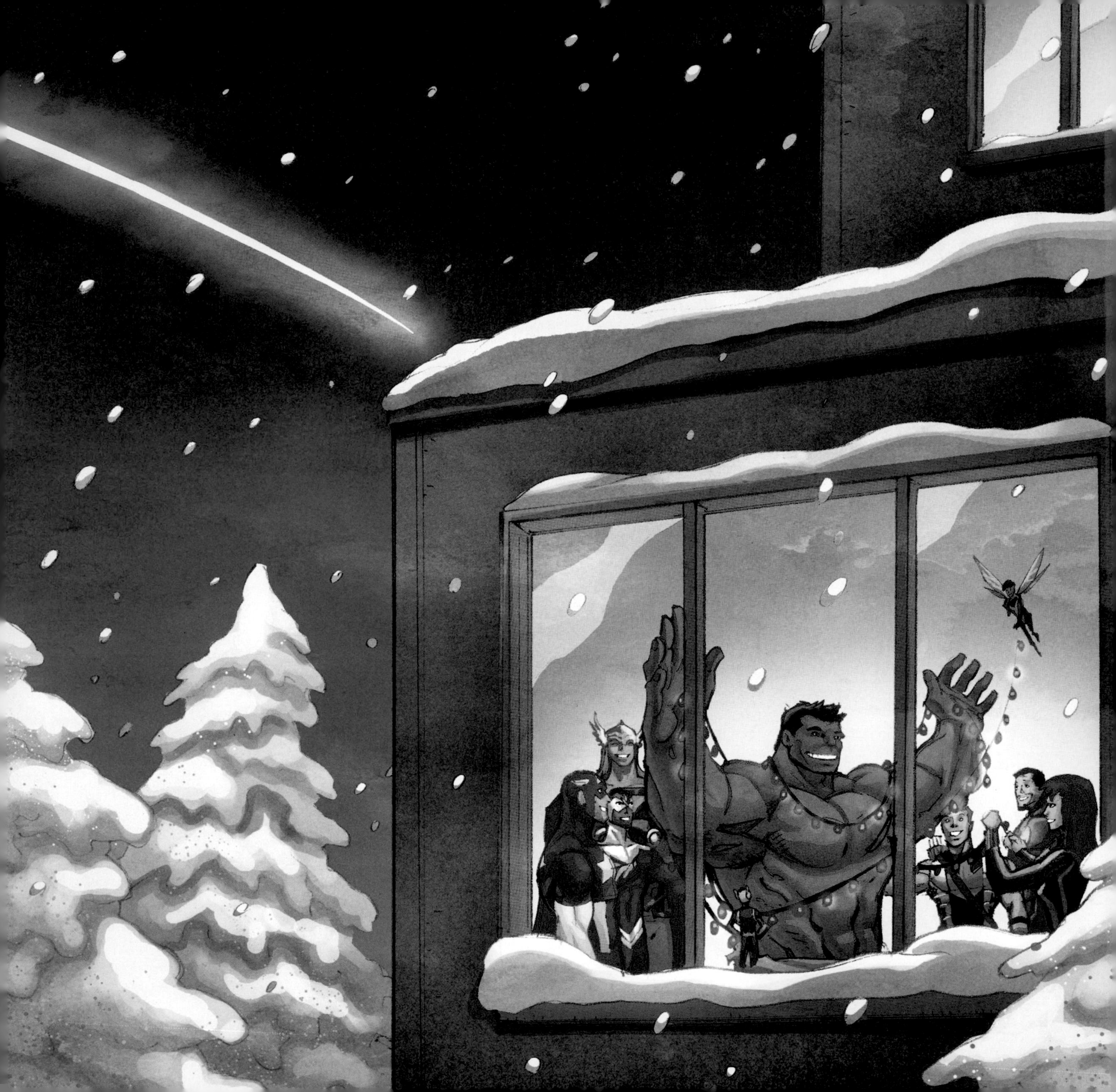

HAPPY HOLIDAYS!

FROM

THE AVENGERS

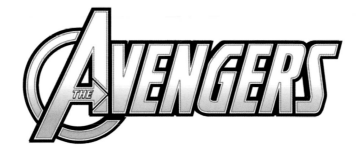

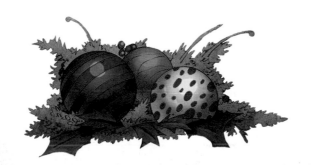